SCALP HUNTERS

BY

ROBERT BROOMALL

As always, for Sharon

Chapter 1

Ignacio Cruz knew the tall rider was trouble from the first moment he saw him.

There was something about the way the man sat his horse — arrogant, challenging — that aroused Ignacio's suspicions. As the man drew closer, those suspicions were confirmed. The rider was in his early twenties, Ignacio guessed. Instead of boots, he wore calf-high Apache moccasins. A deeply furrowed scar, inexpertly — or hastily — sewn, ran across his left cheek, just under the bone. He had dirty blond hair, worn long, and a predatory nose, broken more than once. But it was his eyes that drew the most attention, for they glowed with what Ignacio could only describe as cold fire.

Ignacio Cruz knew about trouble. His small cantina stood on the edge of the *Jornada del Fuego*, the "Journey of Fire," a hundred-odd miles of sun-blasted sand, rock, and thorn along the Arizona border leading to the Eagle Mountains. Ignacio's well was the last certain water until the mountains were reached. Few travelers came this way, and even fewer came with good intentions — a scattering of unmarked graves behind the cantina gave proof of that. Ignacio had seen many bad men. This man was not bad, perhaps, but he was the kind of man that trouble seeks out — and usually finds.

The tall man halted his horse in front of the cantina and swung from the saddle. Removing his worn Henry rifle and saddlebags, he unsaddled his horse and turned the animal loose in the corral. He raised the well bucket, dipped the ladle in, and took a long drink.

Ignacio moved forward cheerfully. He was a fleshy man in country that did not provide an excess of food. He was friendly to everyone; it was one of the qualities that had kept him alive so long. "*Buenos dias, senor.*"

The tall man turned those cold blue eyes on Ignacio. "See to my horse," he said.

"*Si, senor,*" Ignacio said.

"Be careful with him," the tall man added. "He's got a ways to be rode yet."

"*Si, senor.* I am very careful, always."

The tall man nodded. As Ignacio led the horse to the corral, the

1

tall man went into the adobe cantina, ducking his head at the low entrance.

* * *

After the harsh brightness of the desert, it took Cole Taggart a moment to become accustomed to the dim light inside the cantina. It was surprisingly cool in here. There was a musty smell, and a sheen of dust hung in the air, illumined by a shaft of sunlight that slanted through the doorway.

The owner's heavy-breasted wife was behind the bar. "Can I get some food here?" Cole asked her. "*Comida?*"

"*Si, si,*" the woman replied. "*Frijoles, carne.* I bring. You want something to drink —whiskey, tequila?"

"*Cerveza,*" Cole said. It was too hot for anything else.

The woman went out the back door, to the kitchen.

There was one other customer in the cantina. He sat in a dark corner, idly laying cards on the table before him, a bottle of tequila and a dirty glass to one side. The man's traveling clothes were well cut, his boots and hat of the finest make. He had an open, boyish appearance, though on closer inspection Cole judged him to be near forty. A trim moustache and a tuft of hair just below his lower lip that gave him what Cole thought was a Frenchified look, though Cole had never been to France and, indeed, had only the vaguest idea where that country was. The man flashed Cole an engaging grin, "Afternoon, friend."

Cole nodded.

The man indicated the bottle. "Join me?"

"No, thanks," Cole said.

The man shrugged good naturedly and went back to his cards.

Cole sat at one of the cantina's rough-hewn tables, and the owner's wife brought his food and beer. The woman looked part Apache, which was not surprising. This was Apache country. Probably her Indian blood was the reason the Apaches allowed her and her husband to remain alive, eking out a living here on the edge of the *Jornada.*

Cole ate. The food was tasteless, but it filled him up. The best he could say for the beer was that it was wet.

Hoof beats sounded outside, approaching the cantina. Cole had been expecting this; he had seen dust in the west as he rode in. He did

2

not look up from his meal. In the corner, the well-dressed man poured another drink.

Ignacio Cruz started for the door. "More travelers. *Gracias a Dios*. Business, it has never been so good."

Then Ignacio looked out, and his heart faltered.

There were five men, dirty and unshaven. They were mounted on four horses, with one man riding double. They wore bits and pieces of Army uniform — one had a forage cap; another wore sky-blue trousers; still another had a faded blue jacket with brass buttons. Their saddles were Army issue McClellans, and their horses wore the "U.S." brand. They carried Army Springfield carbines in their saddle sockets and Colt pistols at their hips.

The men dismounted and tied their horses outside the cantina. They examined the animals in the corral. There were only two horses present — Cole's sorrel and a dun gray that belonged to the man playing cards.

"*B-Buenos dias*," Ignacio stammered from the doorway.

The men left the corral and pushed past Ignacio without a word. Their leader, a dark-whiskered, sallow fellow, rattled some coins on the rough bar top. "Tequila," he told Ignacio's wife. He pushed back his battered campaign hat, revealing hair cut short in the military style.

Ignacio's wife, whose name was Maria, set five glasses on the bar. She produced a bottle and started to pour. The sallow-faced man grabbed the bottle from her hand. He drank from it and passed it to the next man, who drank and handed it down the line. They did not return the bottle to Maria. They took turns slugging back the harsh liquor, cutting the desert dust in their throats.

"Damn, that's good," said the one wearing the forage cap. To the leader, he said, "Give me some more, Scully."

Scully slid the rapidly emptying bottle back down the bar, and the man in the forage cap drank.

"So far, so good," said a fellow wearing a grimy gray shirt. "We're almost home free."

"Almost, but not quite," said Scully.

Ignacio had come back from tending the horses, and Scully turned to him. "That sorrel gelding out back — who's he belong to?"

Nervously, Ignacio nodded toward Cole, who continued eating, paying the newcomers no attention.

Scully put down the bottle and walked over to Cole's table. Scully wore a checked shirt in addition to sweat-stained Army trousers and troop boots. He said, "Nice horse you got there, mister."

"I like him," Cole agreed.

"We want to buy him."

Still not looking at the man, Cole forked another mouthful of *frijoles*. "He ain't for sale."

Scully grinned. "Everything's for sale, mister. You just have to know the price."

"I know there ain't no price on that horse. Not in this country. I got a long ways to go, and I can't do it without a horse."

"Now, see, you're wrong about that," Scully said, still grinning amiably, " 'cause there is a price on that horse. It's your life."

Cole paused for a second, then put down his fork. He had known it would come to this, no way around it. He looked up at Scully, and his cold blue eyes narrowed even more than usual. He took in the other four deserters — for that was what they were, men who hadn't been able to take the harsh Army discipline and had decided to run for it. The deserters passed the bottle again and spread out along the bar, hands resting near their pistol butts.

"We need that horse," Scully explained. "Since we got our Army 'discharges,' we been makin' some bank withdrawals, if you follow my meaning. Seems a couple fellas got killed in the withdrawal process, and now we got posses comin' at us from all directions. If they catch us, it's our necks, so we got to keep one step ahead of 'em, and we can't be doin' that if we're ridin' two men to a horse."

"That's your problem," Cole told him, "not mine."

Scully kept smiling. "It's your problem now, son. Bein' flush with cash, as it were, we was goin' to buy that horse from you. But now you can just give him to us — as a present, like. That, or we take him. It's your call."

Ignacio Cruz's heavy jowls trembled as he pleaded with Cole. "*Por favor, senor*, give them the *caballo*. I don't want no trouble. When they kill you, I have to dig another grave, and it is so hot today."

Cole gave no answer. Prudently, Ignacio retreated behind the bar.

Cole eyed the deserters. There was no way he could do what he had come here to do unless he had a horse. There would be no talking these men out of taking his horse, either. That meant a fight. Which meant Cole was going to die, because no one could take on odds of five to one and win. It would be galling to die with his goal unfulfilled, but Cole's training had taught him to be fatalistic.

A fellow with a drooping sandy mustache had edged closer on Scully's right; the man with the forage cap stood to Scully's left. The other two were on the wings, easing sideways to catch Cole in a

4

crossfire. Cole's best bet was to go for Scully first and the ones on either side of him next. With luck he might get two of them — three, even. It was the two on the wings who would kill him.

With a moccasined foot, Cole pushed his chair away from the table and stood. "Take him," he told the deserters. "If you can."

Cole didn't wait for the deserters; he went for his gun first. He cocked his pistol and shot Scully in the chest. As Scully went down, Cole shot the man to Scully's right, the one with the drooping mustache. The room was an explosion of noise and yells but it all registered as a dull roar to Cole as he swiveled to his right and shot at the man with the forage cap. The man shot at Cole at exactly the same moment. Cole hit the man in the left shoulder even as he felt the man's bullet zip past his face. Cole threw himself to the floor as bullets gouged the packed dirt around him. He looked for the man in the forage cap, but he lost a precious second because the man had shifted further left. Cole cocked his pistol and pointed it but he was never going to get his shot off in time. A fraction of an instant before the man fired at Cole, a hole blossomed in his forehead, just under the forage cap's brim, and he fell backwards, his shot at Cole missing. Cole twisted on the floor and looked around, pistol ready. One of the deserters on the wings was down. The other, the man in the grimy gray shirt, was bent over a table, holding his chest. He tried to straighten, couldn't, and pitched forward, knocking the table to the floor with him.

Cole looked to the corner. The well-dressed man stood there, smoke drifting from the pistol in his hand.

The inside of the cantina was wreathed with acrid black powder smoke. The five deserters were sprawled on the floor. Already flies were buzzing around them, landing in the blood that pooled on the floor. Cruz and his fleshy wife looked up from behind the bar, where they had dived when the shooting started. The woman saw the carnage and began to wail. Cruz crossed himself and poured a glass of tequila from the bottle that the deserters had left on the bar.

Cole stood and looked to the well-dressed man. "Don't recall asking for your help," he said.

"Let's say I didn't like the odds," the man replied.

Cole nodded. "I don't enjoy bein' in a man's debt, but I expect I owe you one."

There was a gasping sound; one of the deserters was still alive. It was Scully, the leader. He lay on his back, scraping his boot heels on the floor. The well-dressed man stepped forward, pointed his pistol at

Scully's head and fired. Scully jerked once and lay still.

"That's better," the well-dressed man observed with a smile. "I hate it when there's wounded to be dealt with."

He picked up his bottle and got a fresh glass from behind the bar. He filled the glass and handed it to Cole. "You might want this now."

Cole did. He drank, feeling the fire slide down his throat, feeling it ease him inside.

The well-dressed man poured himself a drink and leaned against the bar, for all the world as if nothing had happened, as if five men had not just died here, as if their bodies were not lying at his feet. Ignacio Cruz and his wife ventured from behind the bar. They looked at the bodies, tentatively at first, then they began rifling them, taking the weapons — which they would probably sell to the Apaches — then taking the valuables and pocketing them for themselves.

The well-dressed man reloaded his pistol, regarding the Cruzes with amusement as he did. "Interesting that they wanted your horse instead of mine."

Cole reloaded his own weapon. "Better horse."

The man grinned in appreciation of that fact, and Cole was stabbed with guilt because, if the deserters had gone after the other horse, Cole might have stayed out of the fight.

The man finished loading his pistol and dropped it into his holster. "What brings you to this part of the world?"

Cole didn't want to answer, but he figured he owed the man that much. "Fixin' to cross the *Jornada*."

The man raised an eyebrow. "Not much on the other side, I'm told."

"The Eagle Mountains," Cole said.

"You on a sightseeing trip?"

"Business." Cole holstered his own pistol. "Hear there's a band of scalp hunters working out of there — Colonel Thomas Ballantine's outfit. Thought I'd join up with them."

"Did you now? Well, there's a coincidence. I'm off to join Colonel Ballantine's scalp hunters, myself."

Cole tried not to show his surprise. "Small world," he said.

"The Eagle Mountains are big," said the well-dressed man. "You have any idea where these scalp hunters might be found?"

"Figured I'd worry about that when I got there. Why, you know where they are?"

"As a matter of fact, I do." The man smiled. "Since we're both going the same way, what say we travel together?"

Cole hesitated. He didn't like traveling, or even working, with other men, and he was already irritated at being in this fellow's debt.

The well-dressed man went on. "They say the *Jornada*'s a dangerous place. If the Apaches don't get you, thirst will. There's only a few water holes at the best of times, and at this time of year, only a few of those have water in them. You better know where they are if you want to make the journey alive."

"Do you know where they are?" Cole asked.

The well-dressed man spread his hands, "I'm alive, aren't I? Now, what do you say?"

Cole gave in. "All right."

"Good. What's your name?"

"Cole Taggart."

The well-dressed man held out a hand. "Glad to make your acquaintance, Cole. I'm Wade Markham."

They shook, and Markham said, "You're pretty handy with a gun for somebody so young. Those the first men you killed?"

"No."

"Really. Mind me asking how old you were when you killed your first one?"

"Fourteen, maybe."

Markham couldn't conceal his surprise. "Pretty young."

Cole shrugged.

"You wanted for anything?" Markham asked him.

"Not around here," Cole said. The he added, "*You* wanted for anything?"

Markham grinned. "Not around here."

"When do we leave?" Cole said.

"When the sun gets lower, and the heat lets up."

"In that case, I'll finish my meal." Cole stepped over the dead men and returned to his table.

By now, Ignacio Cruz and his wife had taken everything of value from the bodies. They knew there must be money in the saddlebags, and they couldn't wait to get at them. Sometimes trouble had a golden lining. In the meantime, Ignacio looked up, sweat rolling down his jowls. His voice had a whiny tone. "*Senores*, these bodies. What must I do with them? There are so many. How do I bury them all?"

Cole kept eating. "Me, I'd use a shovel."

Chapter 2

The *Jornada del Fuego*.

The heat rose in shimmering waves. The sun was suspended overhead like a fiery ball. Nothing moved. Nothing seemed to live in that forbidding wilderness. Yet there was life. There were saltbush and brittlebush and creosote. There were cholla and prickly pear cactus. There were lizards, snakes, birds, scorpions and tarantulas. In the dry washes were mesquite, palo verde and acacia.

And there were men. Two of them, riding slowly.

Cole Taggart and Wade Markham had been on the trail since two hours before dawn. Neither man was sweating. Their sweat had dried up long since. The men themselves had dried up. The heat had sucked the moisture from them. It had shriveled them like prunes. And still it beat down, unrelenting, unforgiving, like a living thing, tearing at them. Trying to kill them.

Markham wore his expensive white shirt open to the chest. Sweat and dirt had turned the collar brown. Even the fierce heat could not blunt his boyish cheerfulness, though. "Where are you from, Cole?"

"Around."

"That's funny — so am I."

"Small world," Cole said.

"Ain't it? And why do you want to join the scalp hunters?"

"Money. I hear the Mexes pay good for Apache scalps. Colonel Ballantine's the most famous scalp hunter there is, so I figure if I go with him, that's where the best pickings will be."

"That the only reason?"

"Could be I lost family to them Apache bastards."

"Payback, huh?" said Markham.

"That's right, and a long time coming. What about you? You look more like a New Orleans gambler than a scalp hunter. What brings you to the party?"

Markham laughed. "Money — what else? But for me there is also the excitement of the affair, the danger. If the Apaches catch you, your death will not be a short one. I guess you could say danger attracts me. I crave danger the way some men crave alcohol."

Cole said, "You talk like you've rode with this bunch before."

"I have," Markham said.

8

"How come you ain't with 'em now?"

"I've been in Santa Fe, spending my hard-earned money. I have an affinity for the good life, and that's something you can't find in the Eagle Mountains."

"How well do you know Ballantine?" Cole said.

"The Colonel? As well as any man can, I suppose — but that's not saying much."

"What's he like?"

Markham thought. "He's a gentleman of some cultivation. Why do you ask?"

"Just wondering. Wondering if he'll take me in."

"I should think he would. Judging from what I saw back at the cantina, you have all the attributes needed to join our band of merry men."

"And if I didn't?" Cole asked.

Markham was cheerful as ever. "Then the Colonel would kill you."

Just before noon, they found an outcrop of rock, and they and the horses lay up in its scant shade. Flies buzzed fitfully, as if the heat had stupefied even them; the horses swished their tails at them without enthusiasm, going through the motions. Cole and Markham watered the horses, then themselves. They had brought extra canteens of water, along with oiled canvas bags full of it, but they were still using it at a prodigious rate, mainly because of the horses. Cole gave Markham credit. The scalp hunter was no water-wasting greenhorn.

Cole said, "How far is this water hole — what did you call it — Dead Man's Tanks?"

"That's right," Markham said. "It's nearer fifteen miles than ten. It'll be a good place to camp the night."

"Sure there's water there?"

"No man can be sure of anything in the *Jornada* — that's why they call it Dead Man's Tanks. But there was water there when I passed through last month."

Suddenly Cole stood. From out of nowhere, a cold chill had rippled up his spine. Deftly, he climbed the rock outcrop, making no noise in his Apache moccasins. Just below the summit, he lay on his stomach, and he peered at their back trail.

Markham climbed behind him, nearly as silent. "What is it?" he asked.

"Don't know," Cole said in a low voice. "A feeling." Carefully, Cole quartered the ground with his eyes.

"You think we're being followed?"

"Something like that. You feel it, too?"

Markham shook his head, looking puzzled. "No. I swear, you sound like an Indian, Cole."

Cole grunted and made no reply.

Cole stared for a long time, but he saw no movement, no dust. The desert looked as vast and empty as ever. At last the two men climbed back down the rocks.

"I guess it was nothing," Cole said. But he couldn't shake the feeling.

Cole and Markham waited in the shade until the afternoon was well advanced, then they saddled their mounts and rode out. But Cole kept looking back.

It was within an hour of sundown when they came to the water hole. Dead Man's Tanks lay in the heart of a fortress-like mountain that rose out of the desert. A steep-sided canyon wound its way up into the mountain, and the Tanks lay near the canyon's head. Cole and Markham followed the canyon's gravelly bottom, climbing steadily.

"What if there's no water there?" Cole asked.

Markham replied casually. "Then, my friend, we are in trouble."

The Tanks were a *tinaja* — "earthen jar," in Spanish. They were eroded cups, or holes, in a smooth apron of granite that caught runoff from the rare desert rains. A large ironwood spread its branches over the Tanks, one of the few signs of life in the canyon. The tree provided shade and prevented the sun from evaporating the water. Grass grew around the edge of the rocks. It grew from cracks in the rocks' granite surface. The whickers and restlessness of the horses as they approached told the men that there was water in the Tanks.

The water was scummy brown and thick with old leaves and green slime. The edges of the holes were lined with bird droppings and molted feathers. Cole and Markham brushed aside the leaves and surface slime, and the dead bugs floating there. While the horses drank, the two men scooped water into their mouths.

The water tasted good.

They camped for the night a ways down the canyon from the water holes. They watered and fed the horses, then allowed them to graze on the little bit of grass around the Tanks. After that, the animals were hobbled in a secluded draw a half-mile off, the way the Apaches did it, so an enemy would not be able to find them and run them off.

Cole and Markham sat by a small fire. Cole had killed a chuckwalla lizard, which he skinned and cooked. The two men ate it, along with some tortillas that Markham had purchased from Ignacio Cruz. Cole didn't think that the chuckwalla would agree with Markham's cultured palate, but the scalp hunter seemed to enjoy it.

The two men roasted green coffee beans in a skillet that Markham provided. They wrapped the roasted beans in their bandanas and crushed them with their pistol butts. Then they mixed the beans with boiling water in their tin cups. They were traveling light — no coffee pot.

As Cole sipped the hot, bitter coffee, Markham pulled a bottle of whiskey from his saddlebags. "Try a shot of this with it. It's real Kentucky bourbon."

"Thanks," Cole said. He held out his cup, and Markham poured in some whiskey. Cole remembered all the tequila that Markham had consumed at the cantina. "You like your snake eye, don't you?"

Markham grinned. "As I said, I have an affinity for the good life."

Suddenly Cole put down his cup. He stood, slipping his rifle from its saddle scabbard and cocking the hammer.

"Somebody out there," he whispered.

Markham went for his own rifle. "Apache?"

"White man," Cole said.

"How do you know he's white?"

"I can smell him."

"Smell him?" Markham made a face. "You sure you ain't part Apache?"

Cole ignored the question, all his senses concentrated down the canyon. The smell was faint. "He's a ways off. Too far to try a shot at us."

"That's reassuring," Markham said, " 'cause we make damn good targets by this fire."

"Stay here," Cole told the scalp hunter. "Keep close enough to the fire that he can see you, but not close enough that he can get a good shot."

Markham look faintly amused. "You setting me up as bait?"

"One of us has to do it. I'm going down."

Cole moved quickly and quietly down the canyon. This was the direction someone must come to attack their camp. The canyon's slopes were crowded with boulders. Cole found one and blended in with its darker form. He squatted in the sand to wait.

He smelled the man coming closer.

He made out footsteps — heavy, cautious — climbing the gravelly canyon floor.

Cole came to one knee, raising his rifle.

The footsteps went past him. Cole could challenge this mysterious visitor, but he doubted that the man had come with peaceful intentions. Even if he had, it was his tough luck for being so stupid about it.

Cole fired.

There was an oath. Then an orange flame split the darkness, along with a rifle shot.

Cole fired at the flash. He rolled to one side as an answering shot whined off the rock next to where he had been standing. Cole's rifle blasted into the night, twice. He heard footsteps hobbling away in the darkness.

Cole waited. It was pointless to follow the man now. If he did, he could walk into the same kind of trap he himself had just set. As he waited, he absently rubbed the scar on his left cheek and he thought, as he always did at these times, how close he had come to death the day he had gotten that scar. Another fraction of an inch, and that bullet would have killed him. He remembered the wound's sudden burning pain. He remembered the masked face of the man who had shot him. He could see it as clearly as if it had just happened.

He remained where he was until dawn. He could remain an entire day in one spot, motionless, under the worst conditions. He was trained to do that. Whoever this visitor had been, he was gone. As the flat gray light spread into the canyon, Cole found the man's tracks.

The man had been big. Real big. Cole found something else. Blood.

There was a noise, and Cole turned to see Markham making his way down the canyon, rifle in hand.

"Did you get him?" Markham said.

"Winged him." Cole indicated the blood stains. "From the looks of this blood, it wasn't enough to finish him." He peered back down the lightening canyon. There was no sign of the man. "I wonder what he wanted?"

"He wanted me," Markham said.

"You? Why?"

"I'm a scalp hunter, there's a standard bounty on my head. Five hundred dollars. He could probably collect on you, too, now, come to think of it. That cantina owner, Cruz, must have heard us talking. He must have put the fellow on to us."

"Comin' out onto the *Jornada* — that's a hell of a risk for a thousand dollars."

Markham shrugged. "Some men like that kind of work. Some men don't know any other kind. They have to take the risks as they come. Scalp hunting's the same way."

Cole nodded, then said, "We got three choices. We can go after this fellow, or we can stay here by the water and wait for him to get thirsty and come to us. Or, we can continue on."

Markham said, "Let's go on. That fellow is probably halfway back to Cruz's cantina by now. I think you ran him off."

"I hope so," Cole said. "Come on. We should have been on the trail an hour ago."

Chapter 3

Cole and Markham rode on.

There was no sense in trying to make up the time they had lost. Time stood still in the *Jornada*. Cole suspected that Markham suffered from a hangover. The scalp hunter must have helped himself to that whiskey last night, while Cole had been waiting for the return of their mysterious visitor. Alcohol could dehydrate a man, though, and dehydration was a dangerous thing in this country.

They were in the heart of the passage now. It was rugged, rocky country, broken only by an occasional clump of creosote. The trail was marked by the remains of those who had gone before, people who, for whatever reasons, had sought their fortunes here. Hopes and dreams, come to nothing in this sun-scorched hell.

There were discarded articles of clothing, saddles dry-rotted in the sun with their stitching burst open. There was a wagon, its once-gay paint faded and chipped. There were warped pieces of furniture, someone's prized possessions, abandoned because they'd been too heavy to carry further. There were boxes of old books, photographs, and other personal effects. There was even a piano.

"Wait!" said Markham as they passed the piano.

Cole leaned on his saddle horn; he was too tired to dismount. Markham climbed off his horse and went over to the piano, which was tilted at an angle and bleached gray from the sun. Markham spread his fingers and pressed the keys tentatively, but all that came forth were a fine cloud of dust and a few *thunks*.

"Too much to hope for, I suppose," Markham sighed, and he returned to his horse.

There were the remains of living things in the *Jornada*, as well. Bones of animals — horses, mules, oxen, a dog — long since picked clean by scavengers. There were graves of men, women, and children — their crude headboards carved with faded letters. Who had these people been, Cole wondered. Settlers, prospectors, soldiers, outlaws on the run. Dreamers looking for new lives, only to come to grief under the unforgiving sun. Most had died of thirst, some probably of hunger. Cole and Markham found human bones that weren't in graves, and they bore evidence of different ends. One skull had a small hole neatly drilled in the front, and a larger hole in the back where the bullet had come out. Another skull had been caved in, cracked like an eggshell, by a heavy object wielded with unimaginable ferocity.

"Apaches," Markham explained. "They enforce the vagrancy laws around here."

"Buzzards must make a good living in these parts," Cole commented.

Markham nodded. "They're the only ones that do."

Cole removed his hat and ran a hand through his dirty blond hair. "Don't know who picked your hideout, but you got one hell of a barrier between you and anybody wants to do you harm."

"The Colonel picked it," Markham said, "years ago. And you're right. We're protected by the *Jornada* on one side, the mountains and the Mexican border on the other. We're damn near untouchable. That's what's kept us in business so long. You'd need a large party to wipe us out, and a large party would never get across the *Jornada*. There's not enough water. The Army's tried to get us once or twice, but they gave up, too. Besides, they got their hands full chasing Apaches."

"How long you been a scalp hunter?" Cole asked him.

"A long time," Markham said. Something came over him, and he seemed to grow wistful. "Sometimes it seems like forever."

"Ever thought about quitting?"

"One day, maybe." Then he grinned. "When we run out of Apaches."

Noon came. There was no shade. Cole and Markham unsaddled their horses and sat in the animals' shadows. After dozing a couple of hours in the ferocious heat, they rose.

"The next water's at a seep spring in the foothills," Markham said. "We won't reach it until sometime tomorrow."

"How do you know where these water holes are?" Cole asked him.

Markham shrugged matter of factly. "Apaches told us — before they died."

Cole tapped the oiled canvas water bags hanging from their saddles. "Running low," he said.

"We won't get any less thirsty standing around here," Markham said. "Let's go."

The two men filled their hats and gave the water to the horses, saving just a swallow for themselves. They started off again, walking the horses for a while, taking it easy on them. Markham had lost some of his cheerful disposition. He was having trouble from drinking so much the night before. But he was tough; he didn't complain. At one point, he swooned, stumbled, and sat heavily.

Cole knelt beside him. "I ought to leave you here, for being so stupid," he told Markham.

Markham grinned at him. "Do that, and you'll never find Colonel Ballantine's camp."

Cole swore to himself. He took Markham's canteen. "This got whiskey in it, or water?"

"Water," Markham assured him.

"I'm surprised," Cole said. He gave the scalp hunter a good long drink of the precious liquid.

The water revived Markham, who smiled at Cole through a screaming headache. "Thanks," he said.

"Yeah," Cole said. He helped the scalp hunter to his feet. Markham winced with pain, and the two men continued on.

That night, they made a cold camp. There was no wood for a fire; and, anyway, neither man liked the idea of a fire out here in the open. They sat beneath the stars. From his saddlebags, Markham brought out a fresh bottle of whiskey.

Cole couldn't believe it. "You got to be crazy. Didn't you learn your lesson today?"

Markham had recovered some of his spirit. "Can't get to sleep without it anymore," he said.

Cole shook his head.

Markham took a drink from the bottle. "Nice scar you've got, Cole. How'd you come by it?"

"Got shot," Cole said. Then he added, "I was fifteen at the time."

"Fifteen?" Markham gave a low whistle. "Who did it — a bad *hombre*?"

"Bad enough."

"Care to talk about it?"

"Another time, maybe."

"Whatever you say." Markham held out the bottle. "Sure you don't want some?"

"No, thanks."

Late the next morning, the two men turned off the trail and entered the rugged hills. Markham said the seep spring was in a box canyon. They made their way up a rocky ledge that led to the canyon's entrance. The horses picked their way with care. Suddenly, from beneath a nearby overhang, came the warning buzz of a rattlesnake.

Cole's horse reared. That movement saved Cole's life. Because just as the animal moved, a bullet hummed by Cole's head, followed by the flat report of a rifle shot.

Cole struggled to control the horse. There was another shot; Cole didn't hear the bullet. Drawing his rifle, Cole threw himself from the saddle and scrambled for cover further down the overhang. He hoped there wasn't a den of rattlers in there. He heard the clatter of hoofs nearby as Markham dropped over the ledge and into a protected trough.

Cole stuck his head up, risking a look. A shot made him duck back down. The shot had come from above them. The weapon sounded like a high-powered hunting rifle.

"See him?" called Markham.

"Not yet," Cole answered.

He looked again. Another shot whined off the rock near him, the chips slicing his cheek. He ducked again and dabbed at his bleeding cheek with a dirty hand. Too close for comfort.

"I saw the smoke," said Markham. "He's in that jumble of boulders just above us."

Cole nodded.

"Could be an Apache, trying to lure us into an ambush," Markham went on.

"Could be," Cole said. "Could be our friend from the other night. Hell, in this country, it could be just about anybody."

Markham said, "We can't stay here in the open. We'll fry up like steaks."

Cole agreed. "Let's flush him out."

"I'll go first," said Markham. "You ready?"

"Yeah."

"All right — now!"

Cole snapped a shot toward the boulders. As he did, Markham broke from cover. He raced upward and to his left. He threw himself behind some rocks and lay there, catching his breath and waiting for the throbbing in his head to subside. Then he got to one knee and motioned Cole to be ready. He reared up and fired toward the boulders.

As he did, Cole broke right. He heard another shot, felt something part the air near him. He dove to the ground near the next cover, a small pile of rocks, and wriggled forward on his belly.

Markham's turn again. Cole covered him. Then it was Cole's turn. They repeated the procedure, moving in a widening semicircle, aiming to come in behind the boulders and catch their adversary between them. Markham was almost level with the man's position now. The unknown rifleman fired at the scalp hunter as he dashed forward. Cole saw the smoke and smiled grimly to himself.

Got you, he thought.

He prepared to move.

Suddenly there came the sound of hoofs. Cole and Markham both ran forward as a horse and rider broke from cover. Cole glimpsed a huge man with a long blond pigtail. The man was built like a beer barrel with a head. There was a bandage on his left shoulder. Cole and Markham snapped shots at the man and missed, then horse and rider disappeared behind a rocky hill.

Cole and Markham ran together. They heard the horse, but the man was lost to sight behind the hill. They waited for him to come into the open again, below them.

"He's big, and he's wounded," Cole said. "It's got to be our friend from the other night."

A minute later, man and horse broke cover. The man galloped away, using his mount recklessly on the treacherous, broken ground. A plume of dust rose behind him.

Cole raised his rifle. He aimed, held his breath and squeezed the trigger.

The distant horse reared and fell, throwing its huge rider. The pigtailed man hit hard, then scrambled for cover as the animal thrashed its death throes.

"Damn," Cole swore.

"What's wrong?" said Markham.

"I wasn't aiming at the horse. You ever see that fella before?"

The scalp hunter shook his head. "If I have, I don't remember it. You going after him?"

"No," said Cole. "Without a horse, he's no threat to us. Go after him, and we'd use up valuable time and water — and we might get ourselves shot into the bargain. If he can get himself out of this, good luck to him."

"How'd he manage to get ahead of us, anyhow?"

Cole had thought about that. "He didn't run away the other night. While we sat and waited for him to come back, he mounted up and headed south. He had this place picked out for an ambush. He took a parallel trail, so we wouldn't pick up his tracks."

"He must know the *Jornada*," Markham observed.

Cole nodded grimly. "He's fixin' to know it a whole lot better."

Markham grinned. "I thought the buzzards looked a mite peckish."

The two men retrieved their horses, which hadn't run far in the heat, and continued on, leaving their attacker, whoever he was, to his fate. Cole had an uneasy feeling that, despite what Markham had said earlier, the unknown rifleman had not been after scalp hunters. He had a feeling that the man's bullets had not been meant for Markham, but for him.

It was well past mid-afternoon when they neared the entrance to the box canyon. Both men's lips were swollen and cracked. Cole began taking wide swings to the left and right.

"What is it?" said Markham.

"Looking for sign. I want to see if anybody's been here before us."

Cole had learned as a boy never to go straight into a situation. Check it out from every conceivable angle before committing yourself.

They reached the box canyon. Markham started in.

"Wait," Cole said.

Markham turned.

Cole said, "Is there another way in?"

"One," Markham told him. "But it would be hard on the horses."

"Let's look at it before we go to the spring."

"Cole, there's no one here, and we're dying of thirst. These animals — "

"It's dying of other causes that worries me," Cole said.

"You got that feeling again?"

"Yep."

The scalp hunter raised his eyebrows in resignation. "I won't argue with you, then."

They rode into the hills around the canyon. They hid the horses in an arroyo and went on by foot, carrying their rifles. They worked their way just below the ridge line, so they'd have a good view of the surroundings but wouldn't be skylighted.

Cole led the way. Markham followed, eyes narrowed in pain because the climb affected his sore head. "You sure this is necessary?" he said.

Cole didn't answer. He moved carefully, quietly, never taking a step till he'd scouted it out. "How far?" he whispered to Markham.

"We should be right above it."

Cole moved downward, following an old animal track. Suddenly he put up a hand. Behind him, Markham stopped.

Cole slipped behind some rocks, then waved Markham forward. From their hiding place, the two men looked down. Below, they saw the seep spring. Surrounding the spring was an oasis of tall cottonwoods and sycamores. There were yellow monkey flowers and bluebells. There was lush deer grass and clover.

There were also men at the spring, getting water.

The men were Apaches.

Chapter 4

The Apaches were six in number. They were painted for war, and they were armed with the latest model rifles and pistols. Hobbled horses grazed around the seep spring. There were more horses than Indians. The Apaches drank alertly, their eyes moving all the while. Lean and wary, they reminded Cole of wolves.

"Netdahe," Cole said in a low voice. "I recognize their paint."

"I've heard of them," Markham said, "They're considered renegades, aren't they, even by the other Apaches."

Cole nodded, never taking his eyes off the Indians at the spring. "They're recruited from other bands, some of 'em. Sometimes Navajos and Mexicans run with 'em, too. This bunch is returning from a raid, that's why they got the extra horses. We're damn lucky they didn't hear the shooting earlier."

At that moment, another Indian, previously unseen, stepped into Cole's line of vision. The Indian was old, seventy if he was a day. He was tall and frail looking, and he walked with an arthritic limp. Cole knew that the Indian's looks belied his true nature, however.

Cole said, "See that old one? That's the leader. That's Nanay."

"Nanay!" said Markham in surprise. "I heard Nanay was dead."

"He looks alive to me. "

"How can you be sure it's him?"

"I know him," Cole said.

Markham turned his head to stare at Cole. "Your knowledge of Apaches is considerable."

"Used to scout for the Army," Cole explained.

Markham turned back to look at the Apaches. "They say Nanay's as bad as they come."

"He is," Cole said. "But he wasn't always that way. He's a Chihenne, originally, a Warm Springs Apache. They're the most peaceable band — or they were. Nanay actually liked white men, until we kicked him and his people off the reservation where we told them they could live forever. Seems some damn fool was afraid there might be a few nuggets of gold or silver up there, and civilization would come to an end if white people weren't allowed to find it. After that, Nanay and Victorio went on the warpath; and when Victorio was killed, Nanay joined the Netdahe."

Markham's gray eyes had come alight. He pulled at the tuft of hair beneath his lower lip in thought. "The governor of Sonora has a standing reward of ten thousand pesos for Nanay's scalp. Well, actually, for Nanay, it would have to be his head, but that's no matter. If we could trap his band . . . "

"They live in Mexico, " Cole pointed out.

"We've been to Mexico before, " Markham said, "plenty of times. Apaches in the States are just about played out, anyway — unless you go onto the reservations." He added, "Not that we haven't done that a time or two."

Cole took a deep breath and let it out before he said, "Don't run out of 'em too soon. I ain't made no money off 'em, yet."

Markham grinned. "I like you, Cole. You're direct. I admire that in a man."

Cole said nothing. During all this time, he had alternated between watching the Apaches and the rocky heights surrounding the box canyon.

"Spotted their lookouts?" Markham asked him.

Cole nodded. "There's two. They're watching the two entrances to the canyon. They weren't expecting nobody to come across the top. Still, we're lucky they didn't see us."

"Think this bunch will camp here?"

"I would."

"What do we do then?" Cole noticed how the veteran scalp hunter was deferring decisions to Cole.

"Stay put. If we move, there's too much chance of them seeing us. We've pushed our luck about as much as I care to. Anyway, we got to have that water."

"And our horses?"

"We can't go back for them. We have to hope they don't smell the water and give themselves away."

Markham said, "In other words, we wait."

"That's it. We wait."

As Cole had predicted, the Apaches camped at the seep spring. They led all but one of their horses away, to be hidden. They built a fire, then they killed the remaining horse. They ate the best cuts, like the liver and part of the intestines, raw, and roasted the rest. The two white men heard them talking and laughing. The Apache lookouts came in from the hills, to be replaced by two more.

All this time Cole and Markham lay in the rocks, sucking pebbles, trying to ignore their thirst. Cole was glad they hadn't brought a pack mule. The damn thing would have raised so much racket, the Apaches would have heard it miles away. They'd have searched the hills then, and they wouldn't have stopped until they found the mule's owners. If they found his and Markham's horses, the same thing would happen. Cole hoped the horses wouldn't be attacked by coyotes, either. He didn't want to be left on foot in this country, like that pigtailed man who'd been tailing them.

The sun set in a blaze of purple and gold. Twilight descended on the box canyon. In the rocks, a chill wind picked up. Markham watched the Apache camp and remarked, "That fire looks inviting, doesn't it?"

Cole snorted. "They'd be just as happy roasting us over it as they are roasting that horse." He was glad the wind was blowing away from the spring, so the Apaches wouldn't smell him or his companion.

Soon it was dark. "We'll take turns on guard," Cole said, fingering his rifle.

"All right," Markham said.

"I'll go first. Can you get to sleep without your bottle?"

"It'll be hard," Markham admitted. Then he added, "Though I'm not sure how much sleep I want to get with Nanay and his friends around."

"You always drink yourself out?"

"Most nights, I do. It started during the war." He paused, looked away. "Some of the things I saw . . . some of the things I did. It was the only way I could deal with it. Plus, you're so keyed up in battle, so excited. Alcohol is a way to relax. Haven't you ever felt like that?"

"Sometimes, " Cole admitted. "There a lot of war veterans among the scalp hunters?"

"Some, " said Markham. "We're like your Netdahe — renegades. We've got a little bit of everything."

"Did you know Colonel Ballantine in the war?"

"No. I mean, I could hardly be expected to. It was a big war."

Cole and Markham stayed in the rocks all night, but neither man slept much. They were too thirsty, too scared.

The Apaches awoke well before dawn. While some built up the fire, others scouted the area thoroughly and brought in the horses. Cole and Markham held their breaths as one of the scouts came near them. But the Apache — a boy, a novice warrior — missed them in the dim light. When the scouts returned, the Apaches ate some more of the horse meat. They filled their water bags — made from the intestines of horses and cattle — and tied off the ends with rawhide. Slinging the bags over their shoulders, they departed. They went out of the canyon the way they had come in, driving their captured horses over the more difficult northern pass.

Cole said, "We'll wait before we go down. They'll be watching their back trail."

Markham hugged himself against the dawn chill. "The plan has changed, Cole. We're going to follow Nanay."

Cole looked at him dubiously.

"You should be happy. Those Apaches are money in the bank for us — a lot of money. Colonel Ballantine will want to hear about this. He'll want to know which direction they were headed, so he can get an idea where their camp is. After that, Perico can take over."

"Who's Perico?" said Cole.

"Our tame Apache — if there is such a thing as a tame Apache. He finds them for us."

"He betrays his own people?"

Markham gave him a curious look. "If you want to call it that. I think he does it for the excitement. Plus, the money keeps him in whiskey. I guess he's no different than the Apaches who scout for the Army — except we pay him better."

Cole looked away. He didn't recognize Perico's name, but that didn't mean much. Apaches, like most Indians, changed their names as it suited them.

The hot sun made its appearance. Cole and Markham waited, but the Apaches did not return. At last the two men stood, stiffly. They worked the kinks from their bodies, then moved down to the spring.

Markham stretched full length on the ground, scooping the cool water with both hands. Unlike the brackish water back at the Tanks, this water was sweet and fresh, forced out of underground streams by pressures deep within the earth. "God, that's good," Markham said.

Cole drank sparingly, watching the surrounding rocks, alert for trouble.

They went back for their horses and brought the animals to the spring. They watered and fed them, then set them out to graze. After going so long without water, the beasts were in no shape for travel yet.

Cole and Markham filled their canteens and water bags. They ate jerky and stale corn dodgers. It was past midday when they started on the Apaches' trail.

"I don't want to get too close to them," Markham said. "The last thing we need is to bump into the rear of an Apache war party."

The Indians' tracks were easy to follow because of the shod

horses they had stolen on their raid. Markham said, "What'll they do with all these horses — the ones they don't eat, that is?"

"Sell 'em to the Mexicans for *aguardiente* and ammunition," Cole said. "When they ain't raiding the Mexicans, they trade with 'em. It's an interesting relationship. They don't want to wipe the Mexicans out, 'cause then there'd be nothing for them to steal. They look on the Mexicans as a sort of farm, to be harvested from time to time."

Markham cocked his head in amusement. "Never heard it put that way. You learned a lot scouting for the Army."

"I kept my eyes open," Cole admitted.

Soon the Apache trail broke up. "They'll scatter, then meet this evening at a pre-arranged spot," Cole said.

They followed two sets of the shod hoofs. The next day, they reached the *tinaja* where the Apaches had camped the previous night. They rested there a while and continued on.

The trail followed a steady southeast course. "No twists, no turns, none of the tricks Apaches usually play," Cole observed. "Guess they ain't worried about bein' followed. Wherever they got these horses, they must not have left any survivors. By the time the Army figures out there's even been a raid, Nanay will be back in Mexico."

Markham had been thinking about something. "The Sierra Negros — that's where their camp must be. The trail leads straight there. I don't think we need go any further. We'll let Perico do the rest. He'll find their camp."

They turned away, heading in a southwesterly direction, back toward the Eagle Mountains. Markham gave Cole a sheepish look. "I must confess, I don't know this part of the *Jornada*. I don't know where the water is. I hope we didn't wait too long to turn off the Apaches' trail."

Cole was unfazed. "We'll get on."

That evening, they camped in a dry wash. Cole found a young paloverde, and they dug near it until they reached water, not a lot of water, but enough to refresh themselves and their horses.

The next day, they continued on. They cut off the tops of barrel cactus and sucked water from the cactus meat with a cane Apache drinking reed that Cole carried. They dug out more of the cactus meat and squeezed water from it into their hats, for the horses.

"You think of everything, don't you?" Markham marveled, examining the drinking reed. "Something else you learned scouting for the Army?"

Cole nodded. "You learn, or you die."

At the end of that day, they left the *Jornada del Fuego*. They were in the Eagle Mountains. Markham knew the way now. The mountains were wild and rugged. The cactus and mesquite at the lower levels gave way to oaks and sycamores, then to cool pines and cedars. Cole was glad he'd come with Markham. He could have wandered in this maze of blind canyons for years before finding the scalp hunters.

At last, Markham brought them out of the high mountains, into a wide, level valley, with a pleasant stream flowing through it. Across the valley, a promontory stuck out of the hills, a natural fortress. On the promontory were the ruins of a Spanish mission.

Cole and Markham rode across the valley. A well-used trail brought them into the hills, then across a narrow rock ledge, like a causeway, that led to the promontory, and the mission. A stone wall guarded the promontory's entrance.

The two men had been seen as soon as they entered the valley, and a crowd of men and women waited for them on the causeway and at the wall's carved wooden gates. The men wore all manner of dress — buckskins, Mexican sombreros, plug hats. Even here, in camp, they went heavily armed. Most of the women were Mexican. All seemed happy to see the newcomers.

"Welcome back, Colonel!" somebody cried.

Cole looked over at his companion, and an icy finger of apprehension touched his heart. "Colonel?" he said.

Markham flashed his boyish grin. "Yes. Forgive me, Cole, but my real name isn't Markham. It's Ballantine. Thomas Ballantine. I couldn't tell you right away, I had to be sure you were all right. For all I knew, you might have come here to kill me."

Cole forced himself to smile, as at a good joke — forced himself because killing Ballantine was exactly what he had come here to do.

Chapter 5

Ballantine went on, apologetic. "Actually, there's five *thousand* dollars on my head — not five hundred, like I told you before. That's a powerful incentive for any man. You might have been a bounty hunter for all I knew."

Five thousand dollars was more than Cole had earned in his whole life up to now, probably more than he would ever earn. He had known about the bounty, but this was a job he had intended to do for free, and happy for the opportunity. He could have kicked himself. Fate had thrown Ballantine right in his lap, and he had missed his chance. It would have been so easy.

And now . . .

And now Cole didn't know what he'd do. There was a new consideration. He'd grown to like Markham — or Ballantine, or whoever the hell he was — on the journey here. Not only that, but Ballantine had saved Cole's life. How do you kill a man who's saved your life?

He forced a grin at Ballantine. "Guess you put one over on me."

Ballantine laughed again and turned to the crowd. "This is my friend, Cole Taggart. He wants to be a scalp hunter. I believe he'll be a good addition to the group."

There were a few muttered words of greeting for Cole, then a female voice rang out. "Thomas!"

A pretty, dark-haired young woman pushed her way through the crowd and ran up to Ballantine with her open arms. The two of them kissed. The woman looked to be part Mexican and part Indian. She wore tiers of jangling bracelets and necklaces. The smell of perfume wafted from her.

Ballantine kissed her again, then held her at arm's length. "Elena, how have you been?"

"Better, now that you are here," she pouted.

"Miss me?"

"You know that I did."

Ballantine — it was hard to think of him as Ballantine, and not Markham — kissed her a third time. "Wait till you see what I brought you from Santa Fe," he said. Then he turned. "Come on, Cole."

The two men walked their horses through the mission gates,

accompanied by the woman Elena. They halted in front of the church. The church was maybe a hundred and fifty years old, Cole guessed. It, and the buildings surrounding it, had fallen into a state of considerable disrepair. As a Mexican boy came up to take the horses, Ballantine put an arm around the woman's shoulder. "Elena, this is Cole."

The woman's dark eyes met Cole's. "Hello, Cole."

Cole touched his hat brim. "Ma'am."

"Make yourself at home, Cole," Ballantine said expansively. "Elena and I have some — " he winked — "catching up to do. Pitch your gear anywhere; we're informal here. You and I can talk later."

Ballantine started to lead the woman away when his path was blocked by a wiry fellow, who stood with his head cocked to one side. "Nice to see you back, Colonel."

Arm in arm with Elena, Ballantine smiled at the man. "Thank you, Quirt."

The man called Quirt had a long jaw, high cheekbones and small eyes. His flat-brimmed Spanish hat was tilted well back on his head, revealing unkempt dark hair. He wore leather wrist guards, and a plaited rawhide quirt dangled from his right hand. Part of the little finger on his left hand was missing. He spoke with a deep, flat voice. "Some of the boys been getting restless."

"Been getting a bit restless myself," Ballantine replied.

"Yeah, but you been in Santa Fe, living it up. We been stuck here."

"Nobody said you had to stay," Ballantine told him.

"Any idea when we might be riding again?"

"As a matter of fact, I have. Does the name 'Nanay' mean anything to you?"

"Nanay?" Quirt frowned. "Nanay's dead. The *rurales* killed him last year near Ures."

"No, they didn't."

Quirt frowned. "Says who?"

"Says me," Ballantine told him. "I saw him two days ago, in the *Jornada*."

"What makes you think it was Nanay you saw?"

Ballantine glanced toward Cole. "Mr. Taggart is a personal acquaintance of Nanay's. He recognized him."

Quirt shifted his gaze to Cole. "Did he, now?" He motioned toward Cole with his quirt. "Where'd you find this bird, anyway?"

"On the edge of the *Jornada*," Ballantine said. "I helped him shoot some stray dogs." He gave Cole a conspiratorial smile.

"Why should he be one of us?" Quirt wanted to know. "Scalp bounties ain't been all that good lately, case you're forgetting, and we got us enough ways to split the money as it is."

Ballantine's usually jovial mood grew serious. "He's one of us because I say he is. Do you have a problem with that?"

"I don't like his look," Quirt said. "I don't trust him."

"It's what *I* like that counts around here, Quirt."

The air suddenly became tense. Quirt didn't push it, though. He said nothing, but glared at Cole sullenly.

Smiling again, Ballantine said, "Mr. Taggart will be an asset to our group, I assure you. He's quite a hand with firearms. He also knows the Apaches. Think about Nanay. That's a possible ten thousand pesos in our pockets that we wouldn't have, except for Cole. If Cole hadn't recognized Nanay, we'd probably be getting ready to do another reservation job. Come to think of it, if it hadn't been for Cole, I'd probably be roasting over a fire at the seep spring right now."

He turned to Cole. "This is Quirt Evans. He's been with us from the beginning."

The two men did not shake hands. Cole said, "Easy to see how you got your handle."

Evans held up the plaited leather quirt. Little jagged pieces of metal were knotted at the end of each fringe. Quirt looked it admiringly. "I killed a man with this, up in the Nations. Flayed him alive."

"Gee," said Cole, "you're tough."

Quirt bristled, and Cole went on. "Who was it — some old geezer who couldn't fight back?"

Quirt's lips curled back from his large teeth. "Maybe someday you'll get a chance to find out how tough I am."

"I'm scared," Cole said.

"All right, you two," Ballantine told them. "That's enough." He raised his voice. "Where's Perico?"

A lithe Apache stepped from the crowd. The Apache had a handsome, almost girlish face. He wore a breechclout and a purple calico shirt, with a knife and revolver belted around his waist. Cole breathed a sigh of relief. He didn't know Perico. He could tell from Perico's headband and moccasins that he was a Warm Springs Apache, as Nanay had been.

"*Si, mi Coronel?*" said the Apache.

Ballantine told Perico about Nanay. The Apache's impassive face grew animated when he heard the name of his old chief. Ballantine told him how the raiding party's tracks had run toward the Sierra Negros. "Take some horses and food. See if you can find their camp."

"*Si, mi Coronel*," said Perico. He turned and started for the stables.

Ballantine turned back to Cole. "And now, my friend, if you'll excuse us?"

Ballantine led Elena to one of the mission outbuildings. As the crowd broke up, one of the scalp hunters shouted, "Fandango tonight, Colonel?"

"Damn right," Ballantine told them.

The men whooped.

Meanwhile, Cole set out to explore his new surroundings.

Chapter 6

Cole wandered the promontory and mission grounds. It was easy to see why the mission had been established here, instead of in the valley. There was a well in front of the church, built over an underground spring; and on three sides, the drop was steep, almost unclimbable.

Cole smiled. Apaches prided themselves on their ability to climb. Folks went on about getting up that mountain in Europe, the Matterhorn. If they wanted it climbed, and climbed in a hurry, all they had to do was send for a few Apaches. In reality, this mission was little safer than it would have been in the valley. Still, the location had probably given the Franciscan missionaries and their Pima flocks a sense of security.

Down below, along the stream, was an ill-tended cornfield. Here and there were cattle, several of which were being led up to the promontory by men with long goads, to be slaughtered for the fandango.

The mission church's white dome glowed in the late afternoon sun. The church was long and narrow, with a columned facade. Most of the roof was gone, and the plaster had come off what was left of the walls, revealing the fieldstone underneath. Next to the church was the bell tower. The hundred-pound brass bell was still in place beneath the cupola at the top, still ready to ring the faithful to prayer.

On the church's eastern side was a cloister for the monks. The cloister's wooden columns were in decay, its open grounds overgrown with weeds. There had been an adobe wall around the church, but its bricks had crumbled with time or had been removed to build houses for the Pimas, who had stayed on the promontory after the mission itself had been abandoned. There were numerous outbuildings — kitchen, stables, store sheds — all in ruins.

A century and a half earlier, this promontory had been the site of a flourishing community. Now, it was home only to ghosts — and to the scalp hunters. Some of the scalp hunters, and their women, lived in the abandoned buildings. Others had built crude *jacales* around the promontory. There was even a cantina. The old Franciscans would have been shocked at that. They would have been even more shocked at the filth. The main form of garbage disposal seemed to consist of

31

throwing it off the cliff. Scrawny chickens ran here and there. A goat bawled.

Cole went inside the church, removing his hat out of habit — he smiled as he remembered how the Taggarts had drilled that into him. The old cross over the church entrance tilted crazily. Narrow windows added light to that provided by the missing roof. Faded frescoes depicting the life of Christ — painted by long-dead Indians — decorated the walls. Some of the scalp hunters were living here. The place reeked of unwashed bodies. A few men had curtained off spaces for themselves. From behind one set of curtains came a woman's giggle.

Hell of a way to treat a church.

Cole went to the corral and got his saddle and gear. He pitched them against an open spot behind the church building. Even after all these years, he couldn't stand sleeping under a roof. Bands of mauve, gold, and crimson streaked the evening sky, softening the long shadows.

"There you are," said a voice. It was Ballantine.

Cole turned. The scalp hunter's leader came up, flashing his boyish grin. Had had shaved and changed into a clean shirt and trousers. Cole smelled liquor on his breath.

"Settling in all right?" Ballantine asked.

"Right enough," Cole said.

"Sorry about that trick I played on you."

So am I, Cole thought. "That's all right. I don't blame you. I'd of done the same myself."

"What do you think of our set-up here? Impressive, isn't it?"

Cole nodded. "How long you been here?"

"About a year and a half. We used to camp in the mountains, about forty miles from here, but the Apaches found us there. They almost got us. They'd give anything to eliminate us."

Cole and Ballantine walked across the rear of the mission grounds. Ballantine was in front of Cole. There was no one else around.

Cole's hand dropped to his knife hilt.

He could jam the knife into Ballantine's back and slip away before anyone was the wiser. It would be easy.

He drew the knife from its sheath. He gripped the handle, drew back his arm, ready to strike. Then he stopped, cursing himself.

He couldn't do it.

He'd come here thinking he could kill a man in cold blood, now he knew he had been wrong. Maybe he should just let bygones be bygones, play along here, then get out when he could.

He eased the knife back into its sheath and removed his hand from it. "How'd you get into this business, anyway?" he asked Ballantine.

Ballantine looked over his shoulder. "Like I told you before, I wanted excitement, adventure. After the war, I couldn't let go. I needed the same kind of stimulation."

"You were a colonel in the war?"

Ballantine nodded. "Had my own regiment of cavalry at the end."

"Kind of young for that much rank, weren't you?"

Ballantine snorted. "Age means nothing. Hell, Custer was a general at twenty-three, and he's the biggest idiot that ever wore a uniform."

They had come out from behind the church and were walking toward the bonfire that had been lit for the fandango. Shadowy figures flitted around it. Not far away, two steers were being slaughtered. "What did you do before the war?" Cole asked.

"I read law, believe it or not. Hadn't been for the war, I'd probably have ended up a small-town attorney, like my father. I might even have been a judge — can you fancy that? But when the fight started, I joined up. I rose through the ranks, and things were never the same after that. Once I'd seen the Elephant, I couldn't go back to the life I'd known before."

"Couldn't you have stayed in the Army?"

"I could, but only as a lieutenant. They cut back ranks after the war. I told them no thanks."

"Then what?"

Ballantine shrugged. "I drifted. I wanted to go to Mexico and fight for the French, but that dust-up ended before I could get there. So I did some scouting for the Army. Then I hunted buffalo — what an awful job that was. I was even a peace officer — which might have been all right, except that I liked the fellows who were breaking the peace more than the ones who were keeping it. Then I heard about this Mexican bounty on Apache scalps. That appealed to me. I recruited some men, and the rest, as they say, is history. What about you, ready to tell me where you come from yet?"

"No yet," Cole said.

"You must have some past."

"I just ain't ready to talk about it."

"Got something to do with that scar on your face?"

"A bit."

33

Ballantine started to say something else, but Elena had seen them and she was coming over. She smoothed her sleek hair, which was rumpled from what she and Ballantine had been doing earlier, and adjusted her low-cut blouse. She took Ballantine's arm, and as she did, her dark eyes met Cole's for the second time that day.

Cole returned the gaze.

"The dancing will start soon," she told Ballantine.

"All right," said Ballantine. He turned to Cole. "Come join the fun."

Chapter 7

Fandango.

The scalp hunters had built their bonfire just down the rise from the old mission church. Crackling logs showered sparks into the night sky. Guitarists and fiddlers played. There was dancing and hollering. Men danced with women and with other men, the designated "woman" of the pair wearing a kerchief tied around his sleeve. The slaughtered steers turned on spits. There were tubs of home-brewed beer and kegs of mescal that the scalp hunters had purchased in villages over the border. They didn't have much contact with the States, both because of the *Jornada* and because most were wanted men. There was probably paper on three-quarters of them, Cole figured, and not just for scalp hunting. This place was a bounty hunter's dream.

Ballantine and Elena danced with the rest. Ballantine's boyish face was flushed with liquor. Elena's breasts flounced provocatively beneath her low-cut blouse. At the end of one song, the two of them stopped in front of Cole. "Come on, Cole," Ballantine urged. "Find yourself a partner."

"Ain't much of a dancer," Cole admitted.

Elena stepped away from Ballantine. "I will dance with you." She held out a bejeweled hand to Cole. When he didn't do anything, she said, "Come on, I won't hurt you."

For a moment, Ballantine looked askance. Then he said, "It's all right, Cole."

"No, thanks," Cole said at last. "Think I'll sit this one out. Don't want to break nobody's toes."

Elena shrugged. "As you wish." She and Ballantine began dancing again.

Cole left the firelight and strolled to the adobe cantina on the far edge of the promontory. Some enterprising fellow had realized how much business the scalp hunters could bring, and he'd built this place for them. Since there was no place else for the scalp hunters to spend their money, they probably left most of it here. The owner probably had more money than any of them, save maybe for Ballantine. Cole wondered where the owner got his stock and how he transported it here.

Cole went in. The inside was crude and dark, lit with a handful of candles. The owner, a squat Mexican, languished behind his plank bar. The fandango had taken away most of his business tonight. In one corner, Quirt Evans and three other men played cards.

"*Aguardiente,*" Cole told the owner.

"*Si.*" The Mexican, sweaty and covered with boils, poured the clear liquid into a dirty glass. Cole tasted it and made a face.

The card players spotted Cole. "Hey, Taggart," said a greasy-faced man named Slocum. "Care to sit in?"

Cole shook his head. "Thanks, but I ain't much on gambling."

Quirt leaned back and studied Cole arrogantly. He spoke with his flat, Midwestern drawl. "How come you ain't at the fandango, Taggart?"

Cole kept his eyes on his drink. "Ain't the fandango-in' type."

Quirt studied the scar on Cole's cheek. "That's some scar you got there, how'd you come by it?"

"Cut myself shaving," Cole said.

Quirt said, "You must have a shaky hand."

"Or a sharp blade," Cole replied. He turned and looked at Quirt. "How'd you lose that finger — picking your nose?"

The room went quiet. Quirt laid down his cards and rose. He advanced on Cole slowly, tapping the quirt in his left hand. He smiled at Cole. It was not a friendly smile.

The blow, when it came, was so sudden that Cole would have missed it if he hadn't been waiting for it. It was a backhanded slash, and if it had connected, it would have torn Cole's face to shreds. Cole stepped back as the metal-tipped leather fringes sliced through the air. Before Quirt could recover, Cole stepped into him, grabbed his right arm, pulled it down, and twisted it behind his back. He stuck a foot on Quirt's butt and propelled Quirt head first into the adobe wall.

Quirt dropped to the floor. He lay there a second, gathering himself. Then he rolled over, reaching for his pistol.

He stopped.

Cole had drawn first. His .45 was pointed and cocked.

Quirt relaxed his gun hand. He climbed unsteadily to his feet, keeping his eyes on Cole. "We ain't finished," he warned Cole.

"Fine by me," Cole replied.

Quirt pushed past Cole and left the cantina.

Chapter 8

Cole came back to the rear of the old church, where he had left his bedroll. Behind him, in front of the church, the music and dancing continued, punctuated by laughter and the occasional firing of revolvers into the air.

Cole wished that he had never come here. For years he had wanted — had longed — to kill Ballantine. And now that he'd met him, now that he'd put a voice and personality behind the masked face that had haunted him all these years, he didn't want to do it anymore. He didn't think he *could* do it. He wanted to saddle up and get out of here and get on with his life. Forget the past.

He listened to the noise behind him. He would get his horse and leave, and by the time the scalp hunters knew he was gone, he would be far away.

He reached for his bedroll, aiming to sling it over his shoulder and head for the stables. Then he stopped.

Someone had been through his things. They'd done a good job, but he could tell. The bedroll straps weren't quite the way he had left them. He knelt and opened his saddlebags. They had been searched, as well.

He looked around. He was alone, or seemed to be. *Time to go*, he thought. He hoisted his saddle.

He heard a noise.

He turned. It was Elena. Looking at him.

"Leaving?" she said.

Involuntarily, Cole looked at his saddle. "I — "

"I should warn you, the promontory is guarded. Even tonight. Anyway, you are being watched."

Cole put down the saddle and bedroll.

Elena said, "Thomas sent me to get you."

"Sent you to get me, or to go through my things?"

A small smile creased her lips. "Both, perhaps." Then she added, "The food is ready."

Cole nodded. "Thanks for the warning," he told her.

The smile grew a fraction. "I do not want to see you get shot before you have learned to dance."

He grinned. Then he said, "The Colonel still don't trust me?"

"He has not survived all these years by trusting strangers."

"What about you — do you trust me?"

The smile became a smirk. "Maybe I have not decided."

Cole accompanied Elena back to the fandango. "Why do you wish to leave?" she asked him.

Cole needed a plausible story. "I'm thinking maybe scalp hunting ain't for me. I thought I was up for it, but now . . . I don't know."

"Leaving could be dangerous," she said.

He gave her a questioning look.

She said, "How do we know you are not a spy, a government agent, come to learn the location of our camp?"

"I may be a lot of things, lady, but I ain't no spy."

She stopped, frowned at him as if determining whether he was telling the truth. Distant firelight reflected off her earrings and necklace. At last she seemed to reach a decision. "If you wish to leave, it is best that you wait. Slip away when you are on a mission. They can't watch you as closely then."

"Why are you telling me this?" Cole asked.

"Maybe I trust you after all."

She turned on her heel, and Cole followed her to the party.

Chapter 9

The next few days on the promontory were quiet, even dull. The men were restless, waiting for Perico to get back. They lazed around, drinking and playing cards. Some practiced target shooting or raced horses in the valley. There were occasional fights. The women, when they weren't drinking with the men, tended the crops and cattle. Cole saw little of Ballantine. The scalp hunters' leader spent most of his time with Elena. Quirt Evans was around, though — too much. Conscious of being watched, Cole kept to himself and tried to look enthusiastic.

He grew bored with waiting. He knew they wouldn't let him have his horse back, not yet. "Think I'll do me some hunting," he told Ballantine on one of the rare occasions that the scalp hunters' leader made an appearance. "If that's all right with you."

"By all means," Ballantine said effusively. "I'll tell the guards at the gate to let you through."

Cole got his old Henry rifle and hiked down into the valley. He thought about trying to make it all the way out of there on foot, but he didn't want to try the *Jornada* without a horse.

He walked fast, to work off pent-up frustration and energy. What the hell was he doing here? Why couldn't he have just gone on with his life? He stopped for water in the shade of some giant old cottonwoods that grew along a bend in the stream.

Suddenly the hair on the back of his neck rose. He felt a chill.

He stepped noiselessly into the cover of the trees.

A few minutes later, he heard hoof beats. Distant, but coming this way. Soon a rider emerged from around the bend. It was Elena.

Cole stepped into her path, rifle leveled.

"Oh," Elena said, startled. She reined in her horse.

"Morning, Miss Elena," Cole said.

"Good morning," she replied, recovering.

Cole lowered the rifle. "Sorry — didn't mean to scare you."

She arched her brows. "Are you always so . . . vigilant?"

"Pays to be vigilant, ma'am, if you want to stay alive." Cole looked behind her. "Where's the Colonel?"

Elena gave a rueful laugh. "Recovering from too much drink."

"Seems like he does a lot of that. Drinking and recovering from it."

Her laughter took on a sad tone. "Yes. More than he should. And it grows worse, I fear. I think his — what is the English word? — *conscience* bothers him."

"Why don't he quit, then? Do something else?"

She held out her free hand in a gesture of helplessness. "I cannot say. As much as he detests this life, there is also something about it that he loves. Something that he cannot — or will not — do without."

A stray beam of sunlight peeked through the trees and glinted off the gold cross around Elena's neck. Cole could see now that she had been crying. She was not like the rest of the women up here, who looked hard as nails. There was a softness, a gentleness about her.

She smiled. "You won't shoot me if I dismount?"

"No, ma'am. I'd be glad of the company."

"You do not have to call me 'ma'am.' My name is Elena."

"All right — Elena."

Cole held her horse, while she swung down, her tiered jewelry tinkling. He let go of the animal, which joined his own at the stream. He said, "What brings you so far from the mission?"

"Actually, I was looking for you," she replied.

"For me? Why?"

"To talk." Her dark eyes looked into his, unsettling him. "You intrigue me, Mr. Taggart — if that is your real name."

Cole raised his eyebrows. "If I'm going to call you Elena, you'd best call me Cole."

Elena smiled and went on. "That scar on your face, it says you have led a life of danger, but you do not seem the type of man to make a living by taking human scalps."

Cole shrugged. "I do what I have to, to get by."

Elena wouldn't accept that. "These men here, they are evil. They are monsters, some of them, especially Quirt Evans. They kill without remorse. But you have goodness in you. I can see that. I can feel it."

Cole scratched the back of his head. "You're one of the few folks who's ever said that."

"What *do* they say about you?"

"Things it ain't polite to repeat around a lady, I'm afraid."

She brightened. "And you think I am a lady?"

"Yes, ma'am. Of course."

She smiled at him. Her dark eyes met his, and there was a tingling along the backs of his hands.

"No one has ever said that about me," she told him. She made it sound like him calling her a lady was the nicest thing that had ever happened to her, and maybe it was.

Cole said, "Colonel Ballantine doesn't feel that way?"

She lowered her eyes. "No."

"I'm sorry." He didn't know what else to say.

She shrugged, the shrug of a person resigned to disappointment.

Cole said, "How'd you and the Colonel get hooked up, anyway?"

"The Apaches were responsible. They raided my village in Mexico. It was a vengeance raid, for something my people had done to them — I don't know what, they're always fighting. They killed everyone they could catch. I was the only one who got away. Thomas and his men found me. Some of the men, like Quirt and Slocum, they wanted to have their way with me, but Thomas would not let them. He would not leave me alone in that country. So he brought me back here with him."

"And you became attracted to him?"

"Did I have a choice? Besides, it was not so bad. Thomas is educated and clever. He is kind, too, when he is not drinking."

"And when he is drinking?"

She didn't answer.

Cole said, "Does he leave you often? I mean, the way he had when I met him."

"Often enough. I know he has his fancy women in Santa Fe. I know I don't measure up to them. I know that if he gets married, it will not be to me. I know that one day he will leave me and not come back. And yet . . . "

"And yet you wait for him."

She lowered her eyes. "I have nowhere else to go."

"Do you love him?"

She looked up, and her eyes met his again, as if searching for something in his gaze. "No," she said at last. "I feel badly. Thomas and I are living in sin, not married. It is against all I was ever taught. Perhaps someday Thomas will take me away from this. Perhaps . . . perhaps someone else will."

Her voice had fallen low. She was very close to him. The smell of her perfume was an intoxicant. They were far from the promontory, far from any prying eyes. It would be easy to take her into his arms. Cole had been a long time without a woman, and this one was damned attractive. But alarm bells were going off inside his head. He wondered if this was some kind of trap. He wondered if she was setting him up. If he wanted to be trusted by the scalp hunters, making a play for the leader's girlfriend was a hell of a stupid way to start.

Elena solved his dilemma. She laid a soft, cool hand alongside his head. "Cole," she murmured. "I like that name." Then she raised up on tiptoe and kissed him.

Cole couldn't help himself. He was carried away by passion. He returned her kisses, tenderly at first, then fierce and hard. She matched him. The patch of woods seemed to be spinning about them, as he bore her to the ground . . .

Chapter 10

Afterwards, he held her and stroked her glossy hair. He felt guilty about what he had done. She was like a scared, trapped animal, desperate for love and going after it the only way she knew how. She deserved a better man than Cole.

Two days ago, he had been ready to kill her if she got in his way. And now?

And now, he had compromised himself more than a man in his position ever should have.

She moved in his arms, resting like a hunted creature that has reached safety. She looked at his bare left arm, took it in her hand. "What is this?"

The letters were small, burned into his flesh: "COLE."

"I did that so I wouldn't forget who I was," he said.

"I don't understand. How could you forget who you are?"

Memories flashed through Cole's mind. Memories of a five-year-old boy exploring in the rocks while his family broke camp. Memories of gunshots, screams, of seeing his mother, father, brother, and sister violated and murdered, of watching helplessly while it went on. Memories of the laughter and cries of the bandits as they rode away. Memories of that five-year-old boy standing in the remains of the camp. Standing all day . . .

Then the Apaches came. They rode in silently, taking in the scene, their fierce faces painted. Cole was terrified, but he would not let them see that. He stood straight, fighting back tears and sobs of fear as the Indians rode around him. The Apache's leader slipped off his horse. He walked over to Cole, examining him while the boy fought to keep his lip from trembling. Then the Apache picked Cole up and sat him on the back of his own horse. He remounted and the Indians rode away.

They had taken Cole back to their camp. They had fed him there, treated him like one of their own, and the leader, whose name was Loco, had adopted him as his own son, to replace a son killed by Mexicans. But Cole was determined never to forget who he really was, and one night he had taken a brand from the fire and burned his name into the back of his forearm. "COLE." He would never forget . . .

But in the end, he *had* forgotten. Cole who? He had no idea what his last name was, who his parents had been, where he had come from. He was Cole, a man with no past and damn little future . . .

"What is it?" Elena prodded. "Why did you need to remember who you are?"

Cole was about to reply when there were gunshots from the distant promontory. Elena sat up in his arms. They both looked down the valley, though they were too far away to see anything.

"What is it?" Cole said.

"There is only one thing it can be," Elena replied, and she looked at him sadly because she knew that he would soon be leaving. "It is Perico. He has found Nanay's camp."

Chapter 11

The column of men wound through the rugged fastness of the Sierra Negros. The narrow trail was surrounded by steep, pine-clad ridges and jutting boulders. The crisp coolness of the mountains was a welcome relief from the torrid heat of the desert.

It was late afternoon. The men had been riding since dawn. There were twenty-two of them. They were armed with rifles and sawed-off shotguns. Almost all carried two pistols. If they had been drunk and lazy in camp, they were sober and alert now. Their lives depended on it.

They rode single file, with their equipment tied down. There was no talking. Thomas Ballantine was in the lead. Somewhere ahead of him was Perico, riding point. Two more men rode rear guard. They were in Mexico now. They had to be on the lookout for *rurales* as well as Apaches, though the likelihood of running into Mexican forces in this wild country was unlikely.

Quirt Evans was behind Ballantine. Cole was behind Quirt. Cole was looking for an opportunity to escape. Quirt was still watching him closely, though — Cole might have to wait till the action started to get away.

Cole's every nerve was alive. This was Apache country. He had ridden these mountain trails before, but in far different circumstances. He had been an Apache then, a *yodascin*, an adopted captive of the tribe. These jutting, pine-clad mountains brought back memories of happier days . . .

Blanco had been his Mexican name — every Apache had a Mexican name. His Apache name meant "Boy Who Waits." He had been happy with the Apaches. There had been some rough-and-tumble fitting in with the other boys, but since he was only five, he had soon been accepted as one of them.

Loco had been a good father. He had taught Cole how to hunt and fish, how to follow tracks and how to cover his own. Soon the memories of Cole's real family faded, and all he had left to remember that life were the letters "COLE" burned into his arm.

He had gone on raids with his father, first as a novice — a horse holder — later as a full-fledged warrior. He had stolen horses. He had killed the enemy.

When he was fifteen — or what he thought was fifteen — the band had been invited to a tiswin *fiesta by a Mexican governor. Loco hadn't wanted to go, he suspected the governor of bad intentions; but there had been the possibility of trade, and the band had too many horses and needed guns and ammunition, so Juh, the leader, said yes.*

In the midst of the fiesta, with most of the Apaches drunk, hidden men had appeared. The men wore masks, and they began shooting the Apaches. Loco died trying to save his family. Cole got away, but not before the masked men's leader had fired a pistol almost point blank at his face. By some miracle, the ball went wide, gouging a furrow across Cole's cheek. Face running with blood, Cole joined the Apache survivors racing for safety in the White Mountains. After a harrowing journey, a few of them had reached their home territory. They had no sooner gotten there when they were attacked by U.S. troops. Cole was about to be killed when one of the soldiers had cried, "Hold it! This one's white!"

Cole didn't want to be here with these men. He'd had no choice but to come with them, though. He was supposed to be a member of the band. Instead of dallying with Elena, he should have lit out, put the scalp hunters' camp behind him. He couldn't kill Ballantine now, no matter what the scalp hunter had done to his family. Ballantine had saved Cole's life; Cole owed him. He wished he'd never gotten into this. He had carried his thirst for revenge for nine years. And now he didn't care — no, he didn't *want* to care — anymore. Let it go. The first chance he got, he would slip away.

Elena had cried when they'd parted, before riding back to the promontory. Cole wasn't a man for romantic entanglements, and he was afraid that she had the wrong idea about him. Why hadn't he kept his hands off her? She was too good for Ballantine, and she was damn sure too good for Cole.

At the head of the column, Ballantine raised a hand. The men halted, weapons ready, eyes searching both sides of the trail. An ambush in this country could be fatal.

Like a wraith, Perico appeared. He wore the same purple shirt, breechclout and red headband Cole had seen on him before. A Winchester repeating rifle was cradled in his left arm. He spoke in whispers with Ballantine, then the two of them rode ahead.

The column waited in silence. Horses' hoofs stamped the ground. Low whinnies were choked off by the riders. Then Ballantine returned

46

and motioned the men forward. Ahead, Cole heard the tinkling of a bell. A dog was barking.

Following Ballantine, the column emerged into a mountain glade. The bright green of the grass was all the more startling because they had not seen it in so long. Wildflowers dotted the glade in splashes of red and yellow.

Farther up the glade was a flock of white sheep, guarded by a mongrel dog that was barking at the newcomers. To the other side was a wooden hut. In front of the hut, three children — two girls and a boy — were kicking an old tin can. A heavy-set woman rolled tortillas on a flat stone. The children stopped playing and looked at the newcomers with curiosity. The woman stood, worried by the sight of so many heavily armed men.

Down the hill came the shepherd. He wore ragged pants and *guaraches*, the Mexican sandals. A straw hat hung behind his head by a cord. The mongrel dog came with him, growling at Ballantine and his men. The hair on the dog's back stood up in warning.

The shepherd saw the column's Indian scout. He thought these must be *gringo* soldiers in civilian clothes, crossing the border after Apaches, as had happened several times before.

"*Buenos dias, senores,*" he said, smiling and revealing a mouth missing half its teeth.

Ballantine nodded politely. "*Buenos dias.*" He motioned to Perico, who rode ahead. Quirt eased his horse alongside Ballantine's. A sawed-off shotgun lay across Quirt's saddle.

Ballantine spoke to the shepherd in passable Spanish. "We're looking for Apaches. Are there any around?"

The shepherd waved his arm. "*Mas alla,*" he said, meaning, "further on." "*Mas alla.*"

Ballantine nodded and looked around. The dog watched the newcomers from a crouch, still growling. Ballantine said, "Are you all alone up here, *mi amigo?*"

The shepherd shrugged. "*Si.* We travel with the seasons. We come here for the hot months. In the cold times, we go down below."

"You don't worry about the Apaches?"

"No, *senor*. We know them. They visit us from time to time. We give them a sheep — or they steal it. But they do not bother us."

"You're lucky."

"I don't know about that, *senor*. We put our trust in the Lord. It is all that a man can do."

Ballantine said, "There is no one else with you?"

"No, *senor*. My brother, he used to travel with us, but he married a girl from Oputo. She did not like our life, I think, and now he owns a cantina there."

Ballantine laughed. "Then he's even luckier than you are." He turned. "All right, boys."

As he spoke, Quirt lifted the shotgun and fired both barrels into the shepherd's chest. There was an instant of startled surprise in the shepherd's eyes, then he fell on his back, with the upper half of his body torn apart.

The dog snarled and launched itself into the air, sinking its teeth into Quirt's left arm, knocking him from the saddle onto the ground.

The shepherd's wife dropped her tortillas in the dirt. She started instinctively for her children. "Run, *ninos!*" She was ridden down from behind by a laughing scalp hunter. He fired a pistol into her back and she sprawled forward, flopping in the long grass.

Quirt and the dog rolled on the ground. The dog tore at Quirt's arm. Yelling obscenities, Quirt managed to draw his knife from his belt. He plunged it into the dog's side. Again and again he struck, until the beast let go and dropped to its side on the ground, panting in its death throes.

The shepherd's three children ran for the safety of the pine forest. Yelling scalp hunters pursued them.

The boy stopped to cover his sisters with a sling. He put in a rock, swung it and let go. The rock hit the first rider squarely between the eyes.

"Ow!" yelled the scalp hunter. He brought his horse to a halt, and he slumped forward in the saddle, holding his head. Blood trickled between his fingers. "Shit!" he said.

As the boy fitted another rock to his sling, the next scalp hunter rode by, shooting the boy twice with a pistol. The boy spun and fell on his face.

The youngest girl was running through the long grass when she was shot in the back of the head. She went down without a cry.

The oldest girl was twelve. She was tall for her age, just developing breasts. She had almost made it to the trees, when she stepped in a hole in the ground and fell, twisting her ankle. She hobbled back to her feet, but before she could go further, a lariat snaked around her shoulders and pulled tight. Slocum, the greasy-faced scalp hunter who'd thrown it, reined in his horse and took a turn around his saddle horn with the rope. Helpless, the girl stumbled and fell to her knees.

As she got up, Slocum threw himself from his saddle. He was a burly fellow, with a tobacco-stained shirt. His thick lower lip trembled as he ran up to the girl and lifted the rope from around her shoulders. She struggled, but he held her tightly. He ripped open the front of her cotton dress, revealing her budding breasts. With a little cry of delight, he pulled her to him, feeling her breasts and trying to kiss her.

"No!" said a voice from behind. It was Ballantine.

Slocum looked up. The girl was scared. She looked up at Ballantine, too, as though he were a savior.

Slocum said, "But, Colonel . . ."

"She's a child, you fool," said Ballantine.

"Looks like a woman to me," Slocum said. He turned back to her.

"I said, no!" Ballantine slipped a foot from the stirrup and used it to push Slocum away from the girl. As the girl looked up in gratitude, Ballantine leveled his pistol and shot her in the head. Her arms windmilled, and she fell backward onto the grass.

Slocum advanced on Ballantine angrily. "You hadn't ought to have done that."

Ballantine pointed the pistol at him. "You want some, too?"

Slocum glowered.

"Answer me," Ballantine said. He was in a mood to pull the trigger.

Slocum got control of himself and looked away. "No, Colonel."

Ballantine holstered his pistol. "We're not animals," he told Slocum.

The glade was quiet with the silence of death. The only sounds were the distant bell and faint bleating of the sheep. Wreaths of powder smoke broke up on the breeze.

Ballantine said, "Now, let's do what we came here for." He turned to Cole, all smiles again. "You're the new man, Cole. You want first cut?"

Cole had watched the proceedings, helpless to interfere. It was hard for him to pretend that he was not sickened by what he had just witnessed. It was hard to look disinterested. He leaned on his saddle horn. "No, thanks," he said.

Quirt came up beside him, holding his chewed-up arm. There was blood on his wrist and both of his hands. He was in obvious pain as he said to Cole, "How come you didn't help?"

Cole looked at him without expression. "I signed on to kill Apaches, not Mexicans."

"A scalp's a scalp."

Cole shrugged. "Maybe."

"Sure you ain't yellow?" Quirt asked.

Cole replied. "Was I you, I'd be more worried about that dog having rabies."

Quirt paled. Then he turned away, drawing his knife, which was still red with the dog's blood. Quirt said, "Well, I ain't too proud to lift a greaser scalp. Come on, boys."

The five bodies were scalped quickly, expertly. The circular scalps were stretched on little hoops of green wood to dry, then hung from the men's saddles.

Ballantine was in high spirits as the men went about their grisly task. "Looks to me like we took an Apache warrior, his woman and three little ones — at least, that's what we'll tell the authorities in Hermosillo. This is just something to whet your appetites, boys. This is pocket change. The real payoff comes when we get Nanay."

Some of the men cheered.

"What'll we do with the bodies?" asked one man.

"Leave 'em," Ballantine said. "Nobody comes this way except Apaches. By the time the buzzards and coyotes do their work, nothing will be left of this bunch but the bones."

Just then, a scalp hunter wearing a battered plug hat emerged from the shepherd's hut. "Lookee what I found," he crowed. He held up an earthen jug. "I do believe we got us some mescal." He pronounced it "mez-CAL."

Some of the men raised a cry. They got off their horses and started shoving for a turn at the jug, arguing with each other about who would drink first.

Ballantine rode over. He halted the men by the tone of his voice. "Give me that," he ordered.

The men stopped their argument. The plug-hatted scalp hunter handed Ballantine the jug. Ballantine said, "Hold out that arm, Quirt."

Quirt held out the arm that had been mangled by the dog. Ballantine tipped the heavy jug and poured mescal over Quirt's wounds, cleaning them, washing away the blood. Quirt bit back a howl of pain.

To the rest of the scalp hunters, Ballantine said, "Are you people as stupid as you look? Have you forgotten everything I've taught you? Believe me, nobody wants a drink as much as I do. But what good are you going to be against the Apaches if you're drunk? You'll find yourselves being skinned alive."

He hurled the jug onto a rock, smashing it. The men watched

sadly as the pale liquid drained into the earth. In a hurt voice, the man in the plug hat said, "Well, damn."

Ballantine looked around. "Let's get going." To Cole, he muttered, "Some of these people are impossible, but in this business I guess you can't expect much better."

The men mounted their horses, formed up and rode off.

Cole rode just behind Ballantine and Quirt Evans, who had wrapped a dirty bandana around his savaged arm. Cole was a hard man. He had seen a lot in his time, but nothing that had shocked him like this.

There was no question of slipping away now. Regardless of what Ballantine had done for him, Cole had to stop the scalp hunters.

Chapter 12

The scalp hunters camped that night in the mountains. Though it was cold, they built no fires. Jerky, hard biscuit, and corn dodgers was their meal. There was little conversation. Every man's nerves were on edge. They were deep in Apache country, where the penalty for failure was death.

Only Ballantine was in high spirits. It was as if he enjoyed being in this situation. He saw to the guards and the horses. No detail escaped his notice. He patted men on the shoulder, cheering their spirits.

"How are you bearing up, Cole?" he asked just before they turned in.

"Well enough," Cole replied.

"No second thoughts about coming with us?"

"None." That was true. Cole was glad he'd come now. He couldn't wait to finish the job he'd set out to do.

"I didn't think you would have," Ballantine said, and he flashed that boyish grin. "I've seen you in action." Cole noticed Quirt Evans, off to one side, watching them. Then he wrapped himself in his blankets and went to sleep . . .

The white soldiers had taken him to Fort Bowie, where they tried to figure out what to do with him. He spoke only a smattering of English, not much more than his name — "Cole." He didn't know his last name, so the authorities couldn't learn who his family was. There was no record of missing white boys, so basically they had no idea who he was, and neither did he.

Eventually he was sent to live with Henry Taggart, a rancher who had lost all his own children, save for one daughter, to smallpox. Henry, his wife Alice, and their daughter Rebecca treated Cole well, but he had a hard time adjusting to his new life. There was his habit of sleeping out of doors, for one thing. He couldn't stand having a roof over his head. Then he'd started school. He'd never had any schooling, so at fifteen, he was in the first grade. This led to taunts from the other boys in town, who were suspicious of him anyway. He was different, and they didn't like that. "Cole-chise," they called him mockingly.

The most trouble came from Johnny Jackson, the biggest boy in school. He and Cole fought on Cole's second day. Johnny was big and strong, and he could punch hard, but he didn't know how to wrestle, and Cole quickly subdued him — making a fool of him in the process. Later, Johnny and his friends got together and beat up Cole pretty good. Cole bided his time. Then, one night, Johnny Jackson woke up, his brother and sister asleep next to him, and Cole was beside his bed with a knife at Johnny's throat. Cole didn't say anything. He scratched Johnny's throat with the knife point, drawing a ribbon of blood, and left. Johnny never bothered Cole after that. The other boys who had given Cole trouble steered clear, as well.

Henry and Alice Taggart did their best to make Cole feel at home. Cole called Alice "Ma" after a while because that's what she wanted. He took the Taggarts' last name. He got baptized and went to church with them. He got along with Rebecca the best. Becky was two years younger than Cole, and the two formed a bond as strong as if they had been real brother and sister. Cole proved adept at ranching. He was good with horses and cows, and though he didn't have much schooling, he had good business sense. He remained with the Taggarts until he was eighteen, then he left. The Taggarts wanted him to stay — begged him to — but he wouldn't. He couldn't. He didn't think of himself as a rancher. He was an Apache. A warrior.

He went back to the mountains, back to the Dine, *the people. But his band was all dead, and the other bands didn't want Blanco. He wasn't one of the People any more. They gave him new names, though. His Mexican name was Cicatriz — "Scar"; his Apache name became "Man Alone." He could have joined the Netdahe; Nanay would have been glad to have him. Loco had never liked the Netdahe, though, and Cole felt he would be dishonoring his father's memory by joining them.*

So he had returned to the white man's world. He had drifted that world while he worked on what he had planned since the day his Apache family had been killed — getting revenge on the men who had done it, the men who had turned him from Boy Who Waits to Man Alone. He'd done odd jobs to earn money, working at ranches, mostly, though sometimes driving freight or riding shotgun on a stagecoach. He never stayed in one place very long — his Indian past always caught up with him, and people grew suspicious, even fearful, of him. Everywhere he went he asked questions. Who could have killed his family? They hadn't been soldiers, and there had been a lot of them.

From time to time he went back to the Taggarts; but he never stayed long, even though they pleaded with him to do so. He was too restless, too obsessed with revenge.

Eventually he learned about a band of men called scalp hunters, men who killed the Dine and sold their hair to the Mexicans. He learned the name of their leader, Colonel Ballantine. He learned that their lair lay in the Eagle Mountains, on the far side of the Jornada del Muerto. *Cole knew about the* Jornada — *Loco and his men had talked about it, though they avoided it because it was not their territory.*

So to the Jornada *Cole had gone.*

Chapter 13

The next day, the country grew even wilder. At one point, the trail wound along a narrow ledge of rock. Below the column was a sheer drop of hundreds of feet. To their rear, a waterfall plunged out of a narrow gorge, spilling into a greenish pool far below. The thunderous din of the water echoed and re-echoed off the rocks.

In the afternoon, Perico bid them halt. "Not far now," he told Ballantine.

Guards were put out. The horses were picketed. The men grew increasingly nervous. Evans paced back and forth, tapping his leg with his quirt. His left arm was bandaged from the wrist to the elbow, where the shepherd's dog had chewed it. One man started to light a pipe, but Ballantine snatched it from him.

"No," Ballantine said. "Apaches can smell tobacco miles away."

After about an hour's wait, Ballantine said, "Get ready, boys. From here, we go on foot."

The men left the horses in the care of a guard. "Check your weapons," Ballantine told them. "Be sure they're loaded and in good working order. There won't be time to do it later."

Quietly, the men checked rifles, shotguns, pistols. They stuffed spare ammunition in their pockets. They sharpened knives on whetstones carried in their saddlebags. They took last bites of jerky or biscuit. They drank from their canteens.

"Everybody got their masks?" Ballantine asked.

There were mutters and nods of agreement. Cole fingered the mask Ballantine had given him, a sack with eye slits cut out. The scalp hunters wore the masks partly to frighten their victims, partly to conceal their identities and avoid retribution if any of the Apaches escaped. One reason the scalp hunters were so frightening was because no one could put a face to them.

"All right," Ballantine said in a low voice. He motioned with his arm, "Move out."

Ballantine and Perico went first, followed by the others. Quirt Evans brought up the rear. They walked maybe three-quarters of a mile, climbing through groves of white oak and across a rock-strewn hillside. The late afternoon sun cast long shadows. They were high up; the rarefied air was chilly. Then they emerged onto a mountaintop plateau.

The view was breathtaking. Cole guessed he could see for a hundred miles up here, as wave after wave of rugged mountains receded into the distance. The blue sky was a giant bowl around them, clouds scudding through it like ships of war. The plateau was level, or as close to level as anything the men had seen in the last day and a half. It was open, broken here and there by clumps of oak, pine, and cedar. At the edge of the plateau was a gorge. The sheer rock walls at the far side of the gorge were already in shadow.

The small band of men was dwarfed by the sheer immensity of the landscape as they moved across the plateau. At the edge, Ballantine waved them into line. They crept forward, into the cover of trees and rocks.

The walls of the gorge were not as steep on this side. Below, the gorge dropped into a rugged valley, bisected by a stream. Sand flats showed that the stream was shallow. Across the stream were Apache wickiups.

The valley was in shadow. Fires had already been lit down there. Cole counted twenty-six wickiups.

"Call it a hundred and thirty people, more or less," Ballantine whispered. "Big camp for Apaches."

A drum started beating in the Apache camp, or *rancheria*. Even at this distance, the Indians looked extremely animated. Next to Ballantine, Perico said, "*Tulapai.*"

Ballantine nodded and smiled. "They're celebrating their raid. They're doing our work for us."

Tulapai was a fermented drink made from corn, a kind of beer. The Apaches drank it at big parties, along with *tiswin*, their other intoxicating drink, which was made from mescal. Men and women alike drank until they passed out. Drunken mothers even fed the liquor to their babies. These parties were frequently marred by fights, by killings, by riotous sex among people who were otherwise abstemious. Besides the violence, the use of the beverages led to indolence, bad nutrition, and poor health as a result of lying out drunk in all weathers.

Cole had seen his share of *tulapai* parties. He had seen good men turned into raving animals. He had seen men maimed and killed, women shamed, feuds started that lasted until one or both parties were dead, and were then carried into the next generation. It had been at a party such as this that the scalp hunters had massacred his family. Many Apaches — Cole's adoptive father, Loco, among them — thought *tulapai* and *tiswin* were the downfall of the tribe. That was one of the reasons he had not wanted to go to the governor's fiesta nine years earlier. It was the main reason that everyone else *had* wanted to go.

Ballantine made himself comfortable in the rocks. "We'll let them get a snoot full, then we'll go down and give them their haircuts. Perico, find us a way into that valley while there's still light."

Perico moved off, carrying his rifle. More drums were beating below. Cries and songs filtered up to the men on the plateau. Cole could play this part only so far. The Apaches had been his brothers. He couldn't participate in their massacre. Neither could he stand by and watch, as he'd watched the killings of the shepherd and his family. He hadn't been prepared for those deaths; this time he knew what was coming. He had to warn the people down there. But how, while he was being watched? He'd have to wait until dark and try and break away.

Dusk settled over the mountaintops. In the valley, the fires burned high, the drums beat loud. Already men were dancing. It had been a successful raiding party. It was good to celebrate.

Cole was in a screen of pine trees. Slocum was beside him. With bad teeth, Slocum bit on a blackened fingernail as he watched the proceedings below. "Big killing tonight, eh?" he said to Cole.

Cole grunted noncommittally.

Slocum pulled his knife from its sheath and ran a thumb along the edge. "A lot of work for this. Got you a good knife, Taggart?"

"Yeah," Cole said. He wished Slocum would shut up.

"You took scalps afore?"

"I've seen it done."

"Don't worry none. T'ain't hard. It's fun, really, once you get the hang of it."

"I'm sure," said Cole.

"Knife's gotta be sharp, that's the secret. Razor sharp. Takin' scalps with a dull knife is a pure pain in the ass. The other secret is, you don't want to cut too deep — remember that. But you also don't want to go too shallow. You got to get right under the hair line. You draw you a circle — or as good a circle as you can — and when you're done, you just take a hold and pull. Pull hard, though; she won't come off, elseways. I like to brace my knees on the fella's shoulders, myself. 'Course, different folks got different ways."

Cole said nothing.

"You got any problems," Slocum said, "just come to me."

"I intend to," Cole promised.

As darkness fell over the mountains, Perico came back. He'd

found a way down the gorge. Below, the drums thundered. The singing and dancing grew more frenzied. Shadowy figures staggered in front of the fires. There were wild cries. At the lip of the gorge the scalp hunters waited. Some dozed off. By the time the dance was over, most of the Apaches would be passed out or too drunk to walk. They'd never stand a chance.

Cole wanted to sneak away, to get down the mountainside and warn the Apaches. But he couldn't leave before the others. He'd be missed. Ballantine and his men would know who had warned the Indians. Cole might escape the scalp hunters' wrath, but it would mean leaving them free to commit more outrages, and that was something Cole could not countenance. It wasn't enough to kill Ballantine now. He had to eliminate the entire bunch.

The hours dragged on. It grew cold atop the gorge. The trees and rocks offered little protection from the frigid wind. Around Cole, men shivered, complaining under their breaths. Cole waited quietly, motionless, as an Apache would. It wasn't that Apaches didn't suffer from the elements like other men, it was that they were trained from childhood to endure hardship without complaint.

Finally the word came. "Get ready to move."

The half-frozen men rose from their places. They stretched cramped muscles and flapped their arms to warm up. Ballantine passed down the line. "We're going down in single file. Don't lose touch with the man in front of you, or you might get lost. Worse yet, you might fall off this damn mountain. Keep your fingers off the triggers of those weapons. I don't want anyone accidentally firing and letting them know we're here."

They started off, Perico leading the way. Cole was behind Slocum. An ex-safecracker from New York, Harrigan by name, was behind Cole. In the darkness, the men moved downward through the trees. As the trail rounded a bend, Cole silently slipped off to one side.

Behind him, Cole heard Harrigan mutter in surprise at Cole's absence, then there was the sound of hurrying feet as Harrigan and the other men behind Cole closed the break in the line.

Even before the last of the scalp hunters had gone past, Cole padded off to the right, circling around and ahead of them. There was a sling on his rifle, and he placed the weapon over his shoulders, giving him more freedom to use his hands.

Cole could climb or go down a mountain as well as any Apache, and he needed all of those skills now. He had to get to the bottom before the scalp hunters did. The fires below provided vague illumination, outlining rock outcroppings and trees. He moved along the rock from ledge to ledge, praying that his next step did not launch him into space. He slid on the seat of his pants. He stubbed his toes on unseen rocks. He twisted an ankle. He tore the knee of his trousers, and he felt blood trickle down the inside of his leg. At one point, he lowered himself by the limb of a gnarled cedar. He took a step and suddenly found himself dangling, with nothing but air between him and the bottom of the gorge. Carefully, palms sweating, he worked himself back along the cedar limb, until he found footing again. He rested there for a moment.

He turned his head — had he heard noises behind him? Was he being followed? He listened but heard nothing more. It could have been a rabbit, or a mountain fox.

He kept going, moving left, sliding down the hill on his backside, feeling his way, working toward the fire-lit Apache camp. The throbbing of the drums and the wild keening of the singers provided accompaniment to his descent.

At last he reached the bottom. His heart was pumping, but there was no time to rest. Before him, in the reflected light of the fires, he saw the stream and the mud flats. It would be safe to cross the stream there. Instead of firing shots, he would get close to the camp and shout a warning in Apache. Afterwards, the scalp hunters would think that the Indians had discovered the white men's presence on their own. Or so Cole hoped.

He unslung his rifle and moved forward.

Suddenly, a shadowy form stepped into his path. "Going somewhere?" said a deep, flat voice.

It was Quirt Evans.

Chapter 14

Quirt covered Cole with his rifle. Behind the two men, frenzied drumming mingled with dancing, singing and drunken cries in the Apache village.

Cole caught his breath. "You'd have to be a good man to follow me down that hill."

"I am a good man," said Quirt in his flat, deadly voice. "I never trusted you, Taggart — or whatever your name is. I was watching you. I seen you drop out of line. I followed you, even though it damn near got me killed. Now, what's your game?"

Cole knew that as long as he could keep Evans talking, he had a chance to live. He said, "I wanted to get down here early. I wanted to be the one that got Nanay."

"Bullshit," Quirt said. "I can't figure you out, Taggart. You some kind of government agent or something? It's almost like you were trying to warn them Apaches."

"I'm a scalp hunter, same as you," Cole said.

"If you're a scalp hunter, I'm Buffalo Bill. I'd shoot you right now, but the nose would alert the Apaches and spoil the Colonel's plan. Don't you worry, though. Soon as the Colonel and the boys start their attack, you're going straight to hell."

Cole nodded over Quirt's shoulder. "Tell it to that Apache behind you."

Quirt laughed. "That's the oldest trick in the book. If you think I'd fall for that, you're even stupider than you look."

"Suit yourself," Cole said, still looking over Quirt's shoulder. "But in about two seconds, he's going to put an arrow in your back."

By the reflected light of the fires, Cole saw the slightest bit of hesitation on Quirt's face. Quirt sneaked a look over his shoulder. That was when Cole launched himself at the scalp hunter.

Quirt didn't shoot. He swung the stock of the rifle. Cole dodged reflexively. The blow glanced off the side of his head. It hurt like hell. Cole caught Quirt by the waist. Quirt kept smashing down at him with the rifle. Cole twisted Quirt around, grabbing a leg, dragging him to the ground. Quirt lost his rifle in the fall. He jumped on Cole, gnawing at Cole's ear with his teeth, trying to rip it off. Cole twisted Quirt's bandaged arm, the one mangled by the dog. Quirt groaned with pain, and his grip on Cole relaxed.

Cole shook Quirt off. He rolled away, stars still exploding in his eyes from the rifle blow to the side of the head. He tried to get up, but before he could, something was wrapped around his neck. It was Evans' quirt.

Evans twisted the braided leather around Cole's neck. Cole was on his knees. He tried to get his fingers between his neck and the quirt, but he couldn't. He pushed and pulled, trying to throw Evans off. He couldn't do that, either. He tried to hurt Evans' bad arm again, but this time Evans fought through the pain.

The quirt dug deep into Cole's neck, strangling him. Cole lurched forward on his knees, into the muddy shallows of the river. He tried to stand, but Quirt pressed him down. The two men staggered around in an embrace of death.

Cole fought for air, trying not to black out. It was hard to keep his balance. His eyes clouded.

There was one last move he could make. He went limp. The move threw Quirt slightly off balance. That was enough for Cole to roll forward, ducking one shoulder and throwing Quirt over it. Quirt hit the shallow water with a splash. He partially lost his grip on the quirt. Cole broke free. Gasping for air, he leaped on Quirt's back. He pushed the scalp hunter's head beneath the shallow water, holding it down.

Quirt struggled. His feet scrabbled in the mud. His arms and hands flailed the water. Cole leaned on him with all his strength, for Quirt was a powerful man. Quirt tried desperately to raise his head, but he couldn't get it out of the mud.

Suddenly, Quirt's struggles ceased. A mass of bubbles rose to the surface of the water. Cole held Quirt there another minute, until he was convinced that Quirt was dead. He gave the head one last push, then he stood.

He was wet, muddy, exhausted. His neck was scraped raw; his head throbbed. His voice box felt like it was broken from the pressure of Evans' braided quirt. He fell to his hands and knees in the water. He wanted to roll over and lie down, but he couldn't. He had to warn the village. He staggered back up. Then he stopped.

Across the stream, an Apache man and woman stood at the edge of the trees, watching him.

They must have come down here to be alone and heard the fight. They'd probably thought it was two drunken members of their tribe. Now they realized who it was they'd been watching.

Stumbling from the *tulapai* they had imbibed, the Apache couple turned and ran for the village.

"*Indah!*" the woman yelled. "*Indah!*" — "White man!"

Cole stood ankle deep in the stream. This was the best thing that could have happened.

"*Indah!*"

In the village, the drumming and singing came to a confused halt. The dancers stopped.

"*Indah! Indah!*"

People began yelling, running in all directions.

From downstream came a volley of oaths, followed by Ballantine's voice. "Come on, boys!"

Out of the shadows came the masked scalp hunters in a ragged line. They pounded across the stream, yelling. They scrambled up the rocky slope on the other side. Somebody tripped, and his rifle went off.

"No time to surround the village," Ballantine yelled. "We'll have to charge through!"

Then they were into the flat, open area used by the dancers. Rifles, shotguns, and pistols began to fire. There were yells and screams.

Many of the Apaches had continued to mill around the dance area in drunken confusion. These died quickly. Others ran — or stumbled — for their horses. Others sought refuge among the rocks and brush. Still others climbed the far side of the gorge. Some of the men stopped to fight, covering the retreat of their tribesmen with rifles and pistols, with bows and arrows.

Cole followed the scalp hunters into the *rancheria*, powerless to stop the slaughter. He heard women and children screaming, babies crying amidst the gunfire. The scalp hunters ran through the camp, shooting everyone they came to. Men and women were gunned down without mercy. They were shotgunned at close range. They were shot with rifles and pistols. Cole saw a small child, a toddler, trying to get away. She was shotgunned in the back by a man named Kingsley.

Everything was noise and confusion. Some of the brush wickiups had caught on fire. Cole saw one of the scalp hunters spin and fall, clutching his throat.

"Find Nanay!" It was Ballantine's voice. "Find Nanay, damn it! He's worth ten thousand pesos!"

Cole looked around. It was like watching his own family being massacred all over again. For a moment, he wanted to kill Ballantine now and take his chances, but he held off. He wanted more than Ballantine now; he wanted the whole gang.

The Apaches who had stayed to fight were by the wickiups. They fought well, but they were overwhelmed by Ballantine's men. Men shot at each other point blank in the hellish, blood-red light of the fires.

Then the last of the Apaches went down. Ballantine cried, "Don't let any of them get away, boys! They're money in your pockets!"

The masked scalp hunters charged past the wickiups, into the brush, rooting out survivors. One of the gang ran by Cole with a dripping scalp in his hand. There was no one looking, so Cole shot the man. He staggered and fell into a burning wickiup. Grim satisfaction filled Cole's face.

Apache women, children, and a few men were dragged out of the brush. Some were wounded. All were executed, their bodies brought back to the *rancheria*. They were laid in the open area where, a short while before, they had been dancing. The rest of the Indian bodies were collected. Many of the bodies were unrecognizable because of their wounds. They were tossed one atop the other, like cordwood.

When the last of the bodies had been brought in, it was nearly dawn. Ballantine removed his mask and examined the haul by the fading light of the fires. Cole stood near him. The other scalp hunters took off their masks and clustered around. Due to the close-in fighting, many of them were splashed with blood and brains, bits of bone and hair.

Cole looked at the scene. This was his fault. Each body there was there because of him. If he had just fired off his pistol . . . But no, he'd had some crazy plan — what had his plan been, anyway? He didn't even know. It had been unformed, a hazy something on the horizon that, when confronted, turned out to be nothing. He felt physically ill, wracked by guilt. He was more determined than ever. He was going to eliminate this gang, or he was going to die trying.

There had been enough of an alarm that some of the Apaches had gotten away. From the look of things, those who had gotten away had been men, warriors. When they recovered from the shock of what had happened, they were likely to come back here. And they weren't likely to be in a good mood.

"Is this all of them?" Ballantine asked. Cole noticed that Ballantine was shaking. The scalp hunter's leader removed a flask from his coat and took a long pull. That seemed to calm him.

"All we could find, Colonel," answered the greasy fellow called Slocum.

"There must be about eighty here. That means upwards of fifty

63

got away. Looks like we lost most of the warriors, too. Damn, how did they know we were here? A few minutes more, and we'd have bagged them all. What were our casualties?"

"Two dead, five wounded, Colonel," Slocum reported. "Two of the wounded are hurt pretty bad."

Ballantine looked around. "Where's Quirt?"

"Dunno," said one of the scalp hunters.

"Ain't seen him since we left the bluff," said another.

"Quirt!" Ballantine shouted. "Quirt!"

There was no answer. Only the silence of death.

"Oh, well. He'll turn up," Ballantine said. "He's probably got one of their women out there in the brush." He turned to Perico, "Did you find Nanay?"

"No," said the Chihenne Apache.

"What about you, Cole?" said Ballantine.

Cole shook his head.

"Damn!" Ballantine said.

"Maybe he's in this bunch here," said Slocum, pointing to the pile of bodies.

"He'd better be," Ballantine replied. He looked at the sky. "It'll be getting light soon. All right, boys, get to work."

Chapter 15

As gray dawn filtered to the bottom of the gorge, Ballantine's men began scalping the dead Apaches.

Only about ten men got to do the actual scalping. The rest were needed for other duties. The scalpers pulled up the bodies one by one, like so many slaughtered cattle. With well-sharpened knives, they sliced an incision under each dead Indian's hair, then cut a circle around the crown of the head. Men, women, children — all were treated alike. When the circle was complete, the scalp hunters put down their knives, braced themselves, and pulled. The scalps came away with ripping or popping sounds, the undersides covered with blood and gobbets of flesh.

"Put the scalps in this sack," Ballantine told the men, and he tossed them a leather bag. "There's no time to scrape and dry them. We'll do that later, after we get the horses and get out of here."

"What about the bodies?" asked a wiry, sharp-featured Texan named Werdann. Like many of the scalp hunters, he was splashed with dried blood and gore from last night's massacre.

"Leave them for the buzzards," Ballantine told him. "They're only Indians."

Ballantine put out guards against the return of the surviving Apaches, then he turned to Cole. In the darkness he had not noticed the livid bruises that Quirt's rifle butt had left on Cole's face and the side of his head. Now he saw them, and he winced. "What happened to you?"

"Close call," Cole said.

"You look like you're lucky to be with us."

"I am," Cole said.

Ballantine's complexion was wan, sweaty. He took another pull from his flask, then he flashed his boyish grin. "Well, outside of that, what did you think of your first action with us?"

Cole wished that he could tell Ballantine what he really thought about his "action." He wished that he could put a bullet between the scalp hunter's eyes. But he had a role to play — for the moment. So he said, "A very professional job, Colonel."

"Too bad the savages were alerted, or our haul would have been even greater." Ballantine indicated the bodies stacked on what had once been the dance ground. "A lot of old men among them, aren't there? Indians all look alike to me, especially when they've had their heads blown open. Why don't you check through them, Cole. See if your friend Nanay is there. If he is, cut off his head and bring it to me."

"Sure," Cole said. It gave him a way to avoid taking scalps. He knew Nanay wouldn't be among the dead. Nanay wouldn't be caught that easily. He was too wily. If anyone had gotten out of this slaughter alive, it would have been Nanay.

While Cole checked the bodies, Ballantine ordered two more men to dig a grave for the pair of dead scalp hunters. One of the scalp hunters had been killed by Cole, but Ballantine did not know that. Then Ballantine visited his wounded. Three of them had received minor injuries. A fourth had the lower part of his jaw shot away. Someone had bound the man's face with an old shirt, which was already soaked with blood.

Ballantine knelt and patted the man's shoulder. "Take it easy, Paulsen. We'll get you out of here." There was no doctor at the mission; there was no doctor within two hundred miles. The odds on Paulsen surviving were a thousand to one, but Ballantine did not tell that to the wounded scalp hunter.

The fifth wounded man, a youngster named Childress, had been shot through the spine. He was paralyzed from the neck down. Ballantine looked at the boy squarely. "There's no hope for you, Childress. You know that."

Childress blinked his eyes in scared recognition.

Ballantine went on, "We can't take you with us, you'd never make it out of this gorge. And I won't leave you to be tortured by the Apaches."

Childress blinked again. There was resignation on his face, now.

Ballantine pursed his lips. In a low voice, he said, "I'm sorry, son, I really am. But I've got no choice." He stood and drew his pistol. He aimed it and shot the young scalp hunter in the head. The pistol's flat report echoed through the gorge, breaking the dawn stillness.

"Bury him with the rest," Ballantine told the men working on the grave. He raised his voice to those who were taking scalps. "Hurry, men. We can't stay here long. There's too many Apaches that aren't dead. They could come back at any time, and if they do, they won't be in a good mood."

"Colonel!" It was one of the guards, down by the stream. "Colonel, I found Quirt!"

Ballantine walked over, making a point of appearing clam and in control, of not hurrying. Some of the other scalp hunters followed. Cole watched from where he had been pretending to look for Nanay among the bodies. The guard stood next to Quirt, who lay face down in the shallow water at the edge of the stream.

Ballantine turned to those who had followed him. "Get back to work. You've all seen dead men before."

Reluctantly, the scalp hunters trickled away.

Ballantine knelt and turned over Quirt's body."He wasn't shot. There's bruises on his face, marks on the back of his neck. He was drowned. Drowned in one foot of water."

Ballantine studied Quirt's body. "How did this happen? *When* did it happen? And why here? Was he killed before we even got to the village? But that doesn't make sense."

The guard said, "Maybe he chased one of them Apaches from the village this way during the fight, and got hisself drownded."

Ballantine pulled at the tuft of hair beneath his mouth. "Maybe. But it's strange nobody saw him from the time we left the ridge." He sighed and rose. "I guess we'll never know. Quirt won't tell us, that's for sure. Too bad. He was a good man."

At that moment, Cole came up. Ballantine looked at him. "Well — did we get Nanay?"

Cole shook his head. "No. He must have got away."

"Son of a — " Ballantine caught himself. "All right. There's nothing we can do about it. We've got a good haul even without Nanay. Get somebody to help you carry Quirt over to where they're digging that grave."

Cole nodded, and Ballantine walked away. Cole went back to the *rancheria*, where the squad of men was still taking scalps. The scalpers' hands and sleeves were dripping blood. The scout Perico, who as an Apache did not take scalps, stood off to one side, watching dispassionately.

Cole saw Harrigan, the New Yorker who'd been beside him on the bluff. Harrigan looked ill. "Take a break," Cole told him. "The Colonel wants somebody to help me carry Quirt to the gravediggers."

Harrigan stood gratefully. "Safe cracking was nothing like this." He was a short, pinch-faced fellow, the kind of person who looks perpetually in need of a meal. He wiped his bloody hands on his wool trousers, then he and Cole went to the stream and lifted Quirt's body from the water.

"What do you think happened to him?" Harrigan asked Cole.

Cole shrugged. "Maybe he couldn't swim."

They carried the body into the village, Harrigan grimacing under the heavy load. "Could be, somebody had a score to settle with Quirt, and they thought this was a good time to do it."

"Could be," Cole said.

"Where'd you go to last night, Taggart? I lost you right after we started off." He eyed Cole's cuts and bruises. "You look like you fell off the damn cliff."

Cole shook his head, as if laughing at himself. "I went the wrong way in the dark. I missed Slocum — don't know how. I recovered, though, and caught up to the end of the line. I was right behind you when we went into the village."

"We was lucky just to get to the village. You nearly got half the company lost."

"Sorry. Listen, do me a favor, will you, and don't tell the Colonel. He'd skin me alive."

Harrigan laughed. "Don't worry, I won't. Anyway, it worked out all right." Then his eyes narrowed. "Sure you and Quirt didn't settle a few scores?"

"I'm sure. I didn't like Quirt, but if I was gonna take care of him, I'd have done it back in camp, not out here where it could get somebody else hurt."

Harrigan seemed to find that answer acceptable. He and Cole left Quirt's body with the gravediggers, then went back to where the scalpers were performing their grisly task.

"How many of them Injuns did you kill?" Harrigan asked Cole.

"I don't know," Cole grunted. "Wasn't counting. My share, I guess."

"Don't tell nobody, but I didn't kill a one."

Cole looked at him.

"Too scared, I guess. Too something. I just couldn't do it. I wish the Colonel hadn't sent me to take scalps." He paused. "Guess I'm kind of yellow, huh?"

"You're fine," Cole told him. "Why don't you take a break? I'll cover for you."

"Thanks," Harrigan said. "Colonel's took a real shine to you, Taggart. Wouldn't surprise me, you ended up with Quirt's job."

"Whatever the Colonel wants," Cole said. "He's the boss."

As they returned to what had been the dance area, Werdann the Texan flourished his knife, "Ready to do some barberin', Taggart?"

Cole fought back the urge to shoot Werdann on the spot. "I am, but the Colonel told me to report back to him."

Cole left the Texan to his grisly task. Cole needed a way to avoid helping take scalps, so he went back to the gravediggers. They had laid Quirt in the common grave, atop their other three dead companions. "I'll finish up here," Cole told them. "Colonel said for you boys to take scalps while there's still some left."

"Thanks, Taggart," said one of the gravediggers, and they left.

Cole filled in the grave. He was no nearer a solution on how to dispose of Ballantine then he had been when he'd met him on the edge of the *Jornada*, and that rankled him. So far, all he'd done was waste time — and watch a lot of innocent people get killed.

As Cole was tamping the new-turned earth on the grave, Ballantine came by the scalping area. His color was better than it had been earlier; he wasn't shaking. He'd been searching what remained of the wickiups for anything of value. He hadn't found much — a bit of Mexican and American money, women's jewelry, a watch. Some of the Apache horses remained, but they weren't worth taking. "How are we doing?" he asked the scalpers.

Slocum, who seemed to enjoy his work, held up a hank of hair and skin, blood dripping from it. "This here's the last of 'em, Colonel."

"Good," said Ballantine. "What's the count?"

"Eighty-three," said Werdann, hefting the leather sack Ballantine had given them. "You guessed it right close, Colonel."

Ballantine nodded. "One of our best hauls yet. If only we'd gotten Nanay. He would have been worth more than all the others combined. Oh, well, maybe next time. All right, Mr. Slocum. Call in the guards. Get the wounded on their feet. Form up, and let's be on our way."

Slocum wiped his hands on a dead Indian's shirt, then he moved around the perimeter of the village, cupping his hands and shouting, "Guards in! Guards in!" Meanwhile, the rest of the scalp hunters lined up. The three lightly wounded men were assisted to their feet. Paulsen, the man whose jaw had been shot off, was supported between two of his fellows. Ballantine carried the sack of scalps.

As the men lined up, they shuffled across the grave of their dead fellows. By doing that, they hoped to obliterate the grave's traces, so that the Apaches would not discover it, dig up the four bodies that were buried there, and mutilate them.

"Everyone here?" Ballantine asked Slocum.

"Everybody but Robertson, Colonel. He was posted to the west, just beyond that brush there."

Slocum advanced in the direction of the guard post. "Robertson!

Robertson, what the hell are you doing out there?"

There was no answer. Ballantine looked worried.

Slocum advanced a few steps more. "Robertson! Son of a bitch better not be asleep."

"Here he comes," cried one of the scalp hunters near the end of the line.

Robertson walked into the village. There was a strange stiffness to his gait. His rifle was missing. Slocum said, "Robertson, did you get into the *tulapai*? What the hell is —"

Then he stopped. Robertson half-turned, revealing a two-foot arrow in his back. He pointed in the direction from which he'd come. He said, "The Apaches. They're . . ."

Then he collapsed in the dirt.

Ballantine didn't need to see any more. "The Apaches are back," he cried. "Let's get out of here."

Chapter 16

The scalp hunters retreated across the river. Led by the renegade Apache Perico, they reclimbed the gorge. Shots rang out behind them. Bullets smacked into the gorge's rock walls. The Apaches were considered the best shots of all the Indian tribes, and the gunfire made the fleeing scalp hunters move even faster.

"Don't panic, men," Ballantine cried. "That's what they want. Keep together."

The men were tired and hungry — and drunk, those who had been sneaking *tulapai* — but they kept on, propelled by fear. A pair of them helped Paulsen, the man with the shattered jaw. They reached the top of the gorge with no casualties. They began to run across the open plateau.

"Stay in line, damn you!" Ballantine commanded. "You're not rabble."

Reluctantly, they obeyed him. Cole's heart was in his mouth as they neared the dip where the horses had been left. He expected to find the guard dead and the horses gone.

But the horses were there, hobbled out to graze. The guard was relieved to see the returning men. "Thank God you're back, Colonel. Damn, but I was getting spooked. I heard them shots and — "

"Have the horses been fed?" Ballantine demanded.

"Yes, sir. First thing this morning, just like you said."

Ballantine turned. "All right, boys. Get your gear and saddle up. Don't waste time doing it, either."

The men did not need to be told that last part. They threw saddles and bridles on their horses. Ballantine hung the leather bag full of scalps from his saddle horn. Paulsen and the other wounded were helped to mount.

"Everybody ready?" Ballantine cried. "Move out."

The scalp hunters started off. Perico led the way. The others followed at as quick a gait as they could maintain in this rough country. There was a sense of frightened haste, and only Ballantine's presence kept the retreat from turning into a rout.

Around them, the mountains and forest grew unnaturally quiet. The men were anxious. They looked around as they rode, fingers by the triggers of their weapons. There had been no more shots since they had reached the plateau at the head of the gorge. The Apaches seemed to have vanished.

"Where'd they go?" whispered Harrigan, who was behind Cole.

"Don't worry," Cole told him. "They're out there."

The trail took them once more along the narrow ledge of rock, by the waterfall. Paulsen, the man with the shattered jaw, had difficulty remaining conscious. He nodded off for a second, slumped in his saddle, and almost fell from his horse. He recovered, grabbing the horse's reins in panic, causing the animal to lose its footing on the narrow ledge. Man and horse teetered for a second, as if in suspended animation, then they toppled over. They arced outward into the air, curved back in and bounced off the rock walls, then continued their plunge to eternity, their screams drowned out by the thunder of the waterfall.

The scalp hunters watched, mesmerized.

"Hell of a way for a man to learn he can't fly," Cole remarked.

The column continued on.

Cole wondered what would happen if Nanay found him with the scalp hunters. Nanay would think that Man Alone, the *yodascin*, had turned against his adopted people. He would think that Man Alone had betrayed the Apaches for the white man's money, the same as Perico had done. Only in Cole's case it would be worse, because Cole's adoptive father had been a great chief and war leader of the Chiricahua. He wondered what the Apaches would do to him if they took him alive.

He bet it wouldn't be pretty.

Deep in the mountains, the column stopped. They were at the entrance to a narrow defile, one of many they must negotiate on their way back to their base at the mission. The defile's steep sides were a mass of pine trees and jagged boulders. The quiet was almost deafening.

Up front, Perico looked from side to side, his handsome face searching the rugged slopes.

Harrigan murmured, "I don't like this, Taggart. I truly don't."

"Ain't thrilled about it, myself," Cole said. The hair on the back of Cole's neck was standing straight up. Chills ran up and down his spine like they were chasing one other.

Slocum was in front of Cole. Sweat and dirt and dried blood were beaded on Slocum's greasy face. Slocum tried to wipe them off, but that gesture only spread the mess around worse than it had been.

Ballantine walked his horse forward and came alongside Perico.

"See anything?" he asked the Apache in a low voice.

Perico shook his head, once.

Ballantine looked behind him. He didn't like this, either. He knew that Apaches could travel faster on foot in these mountains than white men could on horseback. "There's no choice," he told his men. "We can't go back. We have to go on."

He waved the column forward.

The scalp hunters entered the defile. The only sound was the clopping of their horses' hoofs on the rocky ground.

The scalp hunters kept riding. Deeper into the defile.

At the top of the slope, an eagle suddenly took flight, its giant wings outstretched.

At the front of the column, Perico turned in his saddle, to shout a warning. There was a rifle shot, and Perico toppled from his horse.

Two more shots sounded at the rear of the column. The rear rider was down, as well, thrashing on the ground in pain, blocking the exit to the defile.

Ballantine turned. He yelled something, but his voice was drowned out as boulders came crashing down both sides of the defile. Some of the huge rocks shattered. Others gathered headway, making a thunderous noise in the confined area. They bounced in the air. They smashed into the column of scalp hunters. Just behind Cole, one of the giant rocks hit Harrigan and his horse, turning them into a gelatinous pulp.

Rifle fire began pouring down on the white men. Horses reared, men cried out and fell.

"Ride through!" Ballantine yelled. "Don't stop!"

The scalp hunters tried to escape. Everything was confusion, with men being hit and riderless horses running loose. Smoke from rifles mixed with dust kicked up by the fallen boulders.

Cole made for the far end of the defile. He had to go slowly — men and horses were down everywhere, and the terrain was bad. He passed a scalp hunter whose leg had been caught beneath one of the boulders. The man lay screaming in agony, trying to extricate his crushed limb.

Cole snapped a couple pistol shots up the hillside. There was no chance of hitting anyone — not one Apache had been seen since the fight had started — but it might make the closest Indians keep their heads down. Gunfire echoed off the sides of the pass, along with the screams of men and animals. Ignoring Ballantine's orders, a group of terrified scalp hunters had dismounted and were trying to make a stand. Cole saw one go down, shot in the face. Ahead, he thought he glimpsed Ballantine escaping from the defile.

Cole came to the place where Perico had been shot. Another man and two horses had gone down here, as well, causing a panicked jam on the narrow trail. Cole kicked his horse up the steep side of the defile and went around them. Bullets hummed so close to his ears that he could felt them brush by. Other bullets whined off nearby rocks.

Then Cole was around the jam and through the defile, onto what passed for open ground in these mountains. Just then, his horse was hit by an Apache bullet. The animal reared and fell, throwing Cole.

Cole hit the ground heavily. Stunned, he lay there for a second, then he tried to get up. He staggered around, unsteady on his feet, his balance affected by the force of the fall. His horse was dead. He looked back at the defile. Most of the scalp hunters back there were dead, as well. The Apaches were moving out of the rocks now.

They were running, coming for him.

Cole fumbled the rifle from his saddle scabbard. He couldn't outrun the Apaches. He'd have to sell his life as dearly as possible, sell his life to the people he had been trying to save. Didn't his school teachers call that "irony"? He knew one thing — the Apaches weren't going to take him alive.

The Apaches yelled as they drew close. Then, behind Cole, there were hoof beats. Cole turned and saw Ballantine riding for him, bent low over his horse's neck, firing his pistol at the oncoming Apaches.

The Indians slowed for a second, surprised by this new development. They began shooting at Ballantine. Ballantine reined in his horse alongside Cole. He slipped a foot from the stirrup and offered Cole a hand.

"Get on!" he cried.

Cole put his foot in the stirrup and swung up behind the scalp hunter. Behind them, the Apaches came on again. Both Cole and Ballantine fired at them. One of the Indians stumbled and sprawled on his face. Then Ballantine kicked his horse and rode away. Behind them, they heard gunfire and the cries of the wounded and dying.

When they were out of the Apaches' range, Ballantine slowed his horse. Ahead, the few survivors of the scalp hunting expedition waited for them.

"That's twice you saved my life," Cole told Ballantine.

The scalp hunter grinned over his shoulder. "What are friends for?" he said.

Chapter 17

Besides Cole and Ballantine, only three scalp hunters had survived the Apache ambush — Slocum, the lean Texan Werdann, and a sullen-looking shoulder hitter called Kingsley. They were all shaken. Kingsley wrapped a strip of cloth around his forehead, where it had been gashed by splintered rock. Blood had gotten all over his face, and he wiped it off with his shirt tail. Slocum's greasy face was sweatier than ever. He was so scared, he could barely hold onto his horse's reins.

"No sense hanging around," Ballantine told them. "It won't do those poor bastards back there any good. Let's go, before Nanay comes after us."

He turned to Cole, who sat behind him, arms wrapped around Ballantine's waist. "Cole, you comfortable back there?"

"More comfortable than I'd have been if you hadn't showed up," Cole said. It had taken a lot of guts for Ballantine to come back after Cole. Cole wondered if he'd have done the same had their positions been reversed.

Ballantine waved a hand, and the five men rode off. The riders hurried, fearful of Apache pursuit. At each bend in the trail, at each mountain pass, the men went cold, thinking this was where they might be ambushed again. But nothing happened.

Night came, and the little group made camp. There was no fire, but they were used to that. Supper was cold jerky and water from their canteens. Slocum was so hungry that he ate some of his horse's grain. The guard rotation was set. Cole and Ballantine were nervous enough, but the other three men were terrified. Cole was afraid they would open up at some forest noise or shadow in the dark and alert the Apaches to their whereabouts.

At last it was Cole's turn for guard. It was the darkest hour of the night. Nothing moved save those predators who inhabited the world of darkness. The exhausted scalp hunters slept.

Cole made the rounds of the little camp. All was quiet. Cole returned to where the scalp hunters slept. He stood over them.

He drew his pistol and quietly cocked it.

He pointed the pistol at Ballantine's head. His finger curled on the trigger. It stayed there for a long moment, then he lowered the weapon.

75

His chest was heaving. Sweat beaded on his unshaven lip.

He couldn't do it.

He let down the pistol's hammer.

What the hell was the matter with him? This was what he'd come here for. He hadn't come to have his life saved by the man he'd sworn to kill, though, and that was the problem. If it wasn't for Ballantine, Cole would be dead now — or well on his way to death. Ballantine had taken a considerable risk to save Cole. How could Cole repay that risk by killing him? Ballantine had murdered Cole's Apache family, and Cole had come a long way to avenge that deed. Now he couldn't go through with it. He swore to himself. The scar on his cheek burned. Ballantine had done that, too. Maybe Cole just didn't have it in him to kill a man in cold blood.

He holstered the weapon and went back on guard. He didn't know whether he had done the right thing or not.

The night passed without attack, but Apaches did not usually attack at night. Dawn was their favorite time. Ballantine had the surviving scalp hunters awake well before then. They formed a perimeter around the camp, nervous, weapons loaded and ready.

The minutes crawled by. No shots were fired at the men. No Apaches appeared.

Ballantine held them there until the sun peeped over the horizon. "Let's go," he said cautiously.

The men grained, watered, and saddled their horses, while Cole, who was without a horse, kept watch. When all were ready, they rode out. Cole still rode behind Ballantine. Cole missed that sorrel gelding; the two of them had been through a lot together.

They rode all day. They passed the meadow where the shepherd and his family had been killed. Vultures and coyotes had been at work on the bodies.

"Funny, isn't it?" Ballantine said, looking at the meadow. "We went to all the trouble of killing those people, then we lost their scalps."

"We did?" said Slocum.

"Yes," Ballantine said with a rueful smile. "Quirt was carrying them. Oh, well. Easy come easy go." He tapped the leather sack that hung from his saddle horn. "We've more than enough here to make up for them."

"And a lot less people to split the money with," Kingsley added.

In the afternoon, the little group of men descended into their home valley. The promontory with the abandoned mission was visible in the distance. The scalp hunters halted in relief, feeling safe at last.

Ballantine said, "We'll stay here the night, long enough to get our women and refresh the horses. Then we're pulling out."

"Pulling out?" asked Slocum in disbelief.

"That's right. The scalp hunters are disbanded, gentlemen. We'll split our take, then it's every man for himself, and it's been nice working with you."

"But why?" said Kingsley.

"Nanay lost most of the women and children in his band. That can't make him happy. He's going to come after us, and he isn't going to stop until he's killed us all."

Werdann, the Texan, said, "But we've got the mission. We can hold it against the Indians, can't we?"

Ballantine said, "With fifty men we could hold that promontory against an army. With five, we can't hold it against the Ladies' Aid Society. Even if we could, we don't have enough men for any more scalp hunting raids. No, boys, it's over. Time to find ourselves another line of work."

He turned to the man who shared his horse. "My apologies, Cole. I hope you got your revenge against the Apaches this time out, because it looks like there won't be any more."

Cole thought about Quirt Evans, and about the other man he had killed at the Apache *rancheria*. He thought about all the scalp hunters for whose deaths he was indirectly responsible. "I did all right," he said.

"We going to Hermosillo to sell our scalps?" asked Slocum.

Ballantine shook his head. "Our first goal is to put daylight between us and Nanay. Hermosillo is back the way we just came. I plan to cross the *Jornada*, then take the long way round, through Yuma, Puerto Penasco, and down the Gulf of California by boat. That agreeable to everyone?"

Slocum, Kingsley, and Werdann looked at each other, shrugged, then nodded. Ballantine said, "Cole?"

Cole shrugged. He was washing his hands of this business. Like Ballantine, he had decided to move on to other things. Once they were across the *Jornada*, he was leaving.

The men rode to the mission. It was a quiet group of women and hangers-on who turned out to greet the little party as they crossed the causeway onto the promontory. Some of the women had started to sob. Their husbands or lovers were missing, and they knew what had happened without being told. Elena walked beside Ballantine's horse, but she had eyes only for Cole, her face filled with relief that he had come back alive.

They rode through the gate into the mission yard, and halted in front of the old church. As they did, a man stepped out of the shadowed church doorway. The man was huge, built like a beer barrel with a head. He wore eyeglasses, and his hair was done in a long blond pigtail that reached nearly to his waist. He carried a Smith & Wesson hunting rifle, and the rifle was trained on Cole.

"Hello, Taggart," he said.

Chapter 18

It was the same man who had tracked Cole and Ballantine across the *Jornada*. There was a faded blood stain on his shirt. He must have gotten that in the encounter at Dead Man's Tanks. It didn't seem to have slowed him down any.

"Thought you was dead," Cole told him.

"Life's full of surprises, ain't it?" said the big man.

Ballantine recognized the big man, too. "You're the one from the *Jornada*, the one who was following us."

"Not you," the big man corrected. He pointed his rifle at Cole. "*Him.*"

Ballantine sounded almost offended. "You were after Cole? Not me?"

"That's right." Behind his wire-rimmed glasses, the big man's eyes gleamed. "There's a bounty on your friend Taggart — one thousand, five hundred U.S. dollars, payable in gold — and I aim to collect it. Been trackin' you a long time, Taggart."

Ballantine whistled appreciatively at the size of the reward. Then he said, "For professional reasons, we're not particularly fond of bounty hunters around here."

"Don't you worry, the rest of you boys don't interest me. I'm kind of a special bounty hunter. Honeycutt's the name. I been hired by Mister Ed Riggins, of Lincoln County, New Mexico, to find the fellow what killed Ed's son, Max."

"You sound more like an assassin than a bounty hunter," Ballantine observed.

Honeycutt shrugged, as if the term didn't bother him, and Ballantine went on. "And you believe Mister Taggart is the man you seek?"

"I know he is. Plenty of boys seen him do it."

"Plenty of boys too afraid of Ed Riggins to tell the truth," Cole said.

Honeycutt went on, "Shot poor Max in cold blood, he did."

Cole said, "That's a lie, Honeycutt. You know it is."

"I know your head is worth fifteen hundred dollars, that's what I know. I got to bring Mister Riggins your head to prove I done the job."

Ballantine sported a wry, almost amused look. "What's this about?" he asked Cole.

"Max Riggins was a real piece of work," Cole said, never taking his eyes off Honeycutt. "Got drunk one night in town and beat up a whore. I told him to stop. We got in a fight. He pulled a pistol, and I killed him. After that, I lit out."

"Sounds like a fair fight. Why'd you run?"

"Max's old man owns the town. No way I'd beat a jury there. It was get out or face a noose."

"And all this over a whore?"

"I kind of liked her," Cole said. "Never slept with her, but I used to talk to her on occasion, when I was in town. She wasn't a bad kid, just havin' a tough time of it. No other way to support herself. Besides, I don't like to see women abused."

He went on. "I guess old man Riggins spread a story about how I was jealous of Max 'cause of this girl, about how she'd turned me down, so I smacked her around and killed Max when he tried to help her." To Honeycutt, he said, "That sound about right?"

"Don't mean squat to me," Honeycutt said. "I get paid either way."

"It was worth it," Cole said. "I'd do it again. Max was a little shit, and his old man ain't much better. I only took the job with Riggins 'cause I was flat broke at the time."

Ballantine still looked faintly amused. "I believe Cole's version of the story," he told Honeycutt. To Cole, he added, "Though I must say it doesn't make you sound like much of a fearsome desperado. I could have hoped for something a bit more bloodthirsty." He drew his pistol and cocked it. He spoke to Honeycutt. "Actually, it doesn't matter what the circumstances of the matter were. As you said, Mister Taggart is my friend." He pointed the pistol at Honeycutt's head. "That means the only thing you're going to collect here is — "

"Hold on." Honeycutt raised a hand. "I ain't stupid, mister. Think I'd of followed you out here less'n I had a hole card to play? You ain't heard the best part." He looked from Ballantine to Cole, letting the suspense build. Back to Ballantine. "Did you know they call your 'friend' here the 'White Apache?' "

Ballantine gave Cole a questioning look.

Honeycutt went on. "Raised by them red devils from a pup is what I hear. Foster father was the old chief Loco."

"Loco?" Ballantine spoke in equal parts shock and surprise. "I remember Loco. We took his hair, him and most of his band. The governor of Sonora paid us to do it. It was our first big payday. Must have been seven-eight years ago."

"Nine," Cole corrected.

Ballantine stared at Cole. "Is what he says true?"

Cole said nothing. Maybe he could have lied his way out of this, but he was too proud of his Apache upbringing to deny it.

Realization washed over Ballantine's face. "If you were Loco's adopted son, you must have been there that day . . ."

Cole sat straighter in the saddle, defiant now. "Maybe you remember a pale-skinned boy about fifteen? You shot him in the face?"

Ballantine scraped the depths of his recollections. "No, I . . . wait a minute. There *was* a kid with blond hair — I remember the hair because when we looked through the scalps later, it wasn't there. I shot that brat almost point blank. Figured one of the Indians must have dragged off the body." He stared at Cole incredulously, stared at the scar on Cole's cheek. "That was you?"

"It was me."

"How did I miss at that distance?"

"Maybe you ain't such a good shot."

"Don't get smart," said Werdann. He rapped the side of Cole's head with his rifle butt. Cole saw stars and fell from his saddle to the ground. Kingsley dismounted and slipped Cole's pistol from his holster, covering him with it.

Ballantine continued. "You told me your knowledge of the Apache came from being a government scout."

Cole lay on the ground. He spit dirt from his mouth. "Guess I lied."

Honeycutt said, "I done a lot of checking up on you, Taggart. Helped me figure out where you might have gone after you killed Max Riggins. One thing I kept hearing is how you was always asking questions about Colonel Ballantine's scalp hunters, asking did anybody knew where you could find them."

Cole regained his feet. He shook his head, trying to clear the cobwebs from it.

"Doesn't seem likely that a fellow raised by Apaches would want to join the men who killed his family," Ballantine mused. "Seems more likely that fellow would be looking for the scalp hunters in order to get revenge."

Cole said nothing. He glared at Ballantine, who dismounted, along with the rest of the scalp hunters. To Cole, Ballantine said, "I don't understand. You've had plenty of chances to kill me. Last night, for instance — there was nothing to stop you. Why didn't you do it?"

"I keep asking myself the same question," Cole said. "Guess I ain't like you, Colonel. I can't kill a man in cold blood."

Ballantine looked at Cole shrewdly, head cocked to one side as he started to put the pieces together. "But you killed Quirt Evans, didn't you? It was you who drowned him in that stream."

"I think of it more as a swimming lesson," Cole said.

"Quirt suspected you from the start. I should have listened to him. And it was you who alerted those savages that we were about to attack, wasn't it?"

Cole stood straight, proud. Why lie about it? An Apache wouldn't lie. An Apache would tell the truth and die like a warrior. Cole wouldn't skulk behind falsehoods. There had been too many of those already. "You figure it out," he told Ballantine.

Ballantine's jaw worked. "If it wasn't for you, we'd have gotten every man in that camp, including Nanay. If it wasn't for you, my men would still be alive. If it wasn't for *you*, we wouldn't be breaking up the scalp hunters. There's a lot of good men's lives on your hands, Cole."

"I wouldn't exactly call them 'good,'" Cole told him. "I doubt there was much of a rush on the Pearly Gates when they died."

Around the front of the old mission church, the girlfriends and wives of the dead scalp hunters cried, "Kill him! Kill him, now!"

Ballantine had become calm again. "I'm disappointed in you, Cole. Very disappointed. And, to think, I saved your life — how many times was it?"

"That weighed on me," Cole acknowledged. "But it still don't excuse the kind of man you are. The kind of things you do."

Honeycutt broke in, speaking to Ballantine. "Told you you'd be interested in what I had to say."

"Most interested," Ballantine replied. "By the way, I must commend you. That was an excellent piece of work to have survived the *Jornada* after we shot your horse."

"I know the territory," Honeycutt said. "Done some prospecting out this way. That was before I learned that hunting men is a sight more profitable than hunting gold. More fun, too."

While they talked, Cole pretended still to be stunned by the blow with the rifle butt. He waited his chance; he knew he would only get one.

To Honeycutt, Ballantine said, "So you want us to let you have Taggart?"

"Just his head," Honeycutt said, lowering the rifle a bit more.

"There's a reward on my head, too," Ballantine pointed out. "On the heads of all these men. How do we know you're not after those, as well?"

Honeycutt said, "Told you — I got no quarrel with you boys. I got nothin' against fellas who kill Indians. Reckon you're making it safer for all of us. No, Taggart's the one I want. Come a long ways to get him, too."

Ballantine nodded, a glint of appreciation in his eyes. At that moment, Cole threw himself at Honeycutt, going for his rifle. He knocked the rifle barrel down. The weapon went off and the bullet went into the dirt. Cole tried to wrench the rifle from Honeycutt's hands, but the big man spun him around and sent him skidding. Cole came back. Before Honeycutt could raise the rifle again, Cole threw a shoulder into his chest — and bounced off.

The big man grinned.

"Shit," Cole said.

Honeycutt tossed the rifle to Ballantine. "Come on, Taggart."

The big man moved in, ham-like fists raised. Cole gave him a left to the stomach — it was like hitting a side of beef — then hit him with his best punch, an overhand right to the jaw.

Honeycutt shrugged it off; his wound didn't seem to bother him at all. He hit Cole two clubbing blows to the head that knocked him backward.

Cole came on again. He ducked a swinging blow, reached up, and flicked off the big man's thick eyeglasses.

Honeycutt groped around, half blind. "You son of a bitch."

Cole stepped on the glasses, breaking them. Then he kicked Honeycutt in the shin. Honeycutt yelped and hopped on one leg. Cole rained blows on the big man's face. Honeycutt lunged forward and hung on, trying to clear his head. Cole tried to push off. Honeycutt hugged him tighter, crushing his ribs. Cole couldn't breathe. At last, Honeycutt let him go. Cole stood helplessly, bent over and sucking in air. He looked, saw what was coming and grimaced. A right hand hit his cheek with the impact of a runaway train.

The next thing Cole knew, he was on his back, seeing double. Honeycutt kicked him in the side of the head. Cole had been kicked by horses that hadn't hurt that much.

The crowd was yelling. Out of the fog of pain, Cole saw Elena looking at him anxiously. Then he saw Ballantine. The scalp hunter had a wistful smile on his face as he shook his head. "Cole. Cole."

Honeycutt found his glasses and put them back on. Both lenses were cracked. Honeycutt growled with anger. He took his rifle back from Ballantine and pointed it at Cole, ready to squeeze the trigger.

Ballantine held out a hand, stopping him. "Wait. I know a better way, if you're open to it."

Honeycutt was breathing heavily, but he looked curious. "I'm open to anything good. All I need is his head in one piece. I figure to pickle it and take it as evidence that I really killed him. Maybe I can exhibit it on the side and make me some extra money. People'd pay to see the White Apache, I reckon."

"Very enterprising," Ballantine approved. "If you'll allow us, then, we'll dispose of him in a more . . . shall we say, *leisurely* . . . fashion." He turned. "Cole, what happened? I trusted you. I *liked* you. Yet you betrayed me."

Cole said, "You make yourself sound like some kind of saint, Ballantine. Cut the fancy talk, and let's get to the good part."

"Oh, it will be good, believe me," Ballantine told him. "Tie his hands, Mr. Slocum."

While Werdann and Kingsley covered Cole with their rifles, Slocum tied Cole's hands behind his back.

Ballantine started away. "Bring him along," he ordered.

Chapter 19

Kingsley and Werdann prodded Cole, none too gently, with their rifle barrels. He stumbled along behind Ballantine. Slocum walked beside him, glowering. "I thought you was our friend, Taggart. Hell, I even offered to help you."

The vengeful crowd of women and hangers-on followed them. Cole tried to look for Elena, but Kingsley, the man with the wounded head, jabbed him with the rifle.

"Keep going, damn you. Because of you, all our friends are dead."

"And we're out the ten thousand pesos we would have got for Nanay," Werdann added.

In front of Cole, Ballantine turned to Honeycutt, the huge bounty hunter. "As our guest, you may choose the method of Mr. Taggart's demise. We only have until tomorrow morning, because we must vacate these premises, so some of the more sophisticated options are not open to us."

"Long as I get his head," Honeycutt insisted, "in good enough shape that he can be identified."

"So you shall. So you shall. Tell me, what sounds better — should we roast him over a fire, or stake him out on an ant hill?"

The bounty hunter stumbled over an empty bottle; he couldn't see very well with his cracked glasses. It was incongruous, a man so big and powerful, with such weak eyes. He said, "I seen a fella roasted alive once, by Comanches — seen what was left of him, anyway — over to Texas. Never seen a man staked on an ant hill. Pretty good, is it?"

"You'll love it," Ballantine assured him. "Mr. Kingsley, fetch a jug of molasses, will you?"

The usually sullen Kingsley grinned and hurried back to the mission.

The scalp hunters led Cole through the gate and off the promontory. Cole's head throbbed from being hit by the rifle butt, but that was the least of his worries right now. He'd seen men staked out on anthills. He knew what he was in for. He knew that, in the end, he'd be reduced to a quivering, screaming mass, begging to die, as the ants ate him alive.

The little procession made its way to a spot near the bottom of the hill. Suddenly Cole broke away, running for the river. With luck, one clean shot would take him out. And, who knew, there was always a chance he'd get away. It would be dark soon. If he could just . . .

There was a rifle shot, and a bullet whined by his ear.

"Don't shoot!" he heard Ballantine cry. "That's what he wants."

It was hard running with his hands tied behind him. Cole stumbled over a dip in the earth. He heard footsteps behind him. The footsteps drew closer. Cole pumped his long legs as hard as he could, but he couldn't outrun his pursuers. Then somebody tackled him, sending him face first onto the rocky ground.

He lay there, the breath momentarily knocked out of him, spitting dirt from his mouth. He tried to get up again, but before he could, a noose was dropped around his neck.

"Drag him," Ballantine said.

Slocum and Werdann pulled on the rope. Cole stumbled to his feet to avoid being choked. The two scalp hunters dragged him along, his Apache moccasins scrabbling on the rocky ground. He couldn't tell where his captors were taking him. All he could see was the ground. At last they stopped. Strong hands grabbed Cole by the collar and threw him to the ground.

The breath was knocked from him again. After a second, he rolled over. His face was scratched and full of gravel. His mouth was bleeding. He tried to think of a plan of action. But before he could do anything, his feet were grabbed, tied, and secured to the ground with wooden stakes, pounded in with pistol butts. His arms and wrists were pulled over his head and secured in a similar fashion.

"There," said Slocum, standing above him.

"That'll slow you down a bit," Werdann added.

Cole twisted his head and looked around. To his left were a series of turned-up ant hills. Red ants ran all over them. Cole's blood froze. Already some of the ants scouted over his shirt sleeve. Something nipped his wrist.

"Damn!" Honeycutt chuckled. "This is going to be *some* good."

The crowd of women was all around, yelling for Cole's blood, wanting revenge for dead husbands and lovers. Cole couldn't smell the tequila on their breaths but he could see it in their contorted faces. He pulled against the stakes that held his hands and feet, but they had been driven in too tightly. The scalp hunters laughed at his futile efforts.

Slocum and Werdann cut off Cole's shirt. "The pants, too?" Kingsley asked Ballantine.

"Heavens, no," Ballantine said in mock horror. "We must observe the proprieties — there are ladies present."

Already ants were running over Cole's naked chest and stomach. He felt their tiny, powerful jaws biting him. A few bites would hurt. They would raise red lumps on his skin. Thousands on thousands of bites would strip the flesh from his bones. He had seen it happen.

Kingsley was back, and Ballantine said, "Mr. Kingsley, if you would be so kind as to apply the molasses?"

Kingsley grinned. He tipped the molasses jug and poured the sticky liquid, using his hand to spread the molasses over Cole's exposed chest, neck, and back.

"Remember — leave the head alone," Honeycutt reminded him.

This admonition occasioned some sadness among the scalp hunters and their women — they'd like to have seen Cole's head eaten off. When Kingsley was done, he wiped the molasses from his hand in the dirt. Swearing, he brushed off as many as he could of the ants that were now crawling all over his hands and forearms. Ballantine motioned, and Slocum cut the rope that bound Cole's hands. He and Werdann each grabbed one of Cole's arms. Cole fought violently, but with his feet pinned, he had no chance. The two scalp hunters dragged his upper body around and dropped it across the ant hills. They stretched his arms to the limits and re-staked them to the ground.

Cole looked up. The light was failing. There were already torches in the crowd. Some of the women squatted, spitting at him, hurling invective, getting ready to enjoy the show. They had tequila and tortillas, and blankets to wrap around themselves. They intended to spend the night, to watch the whole thing. Cole looked around, but he didn't see Elena.

Disturbed by this huge alien presence and attracted by the sweet molasses, the red ants boiled out of their mounds. The ants swarmed over Cole's chest and neck. They got into his trousers, into his hair. He closed his eyes. *Please, God*, he thought, *don't let them get in my eyes.* In no time, he was covered with ants. He felt like he was on fire. He struggled against his bonds. He tried to shake them off. It was no good. He was held tight.

More and more ants came, uncounted numbers of them. Their jaws dug into Cole like thousands of fiery needle pricks. Around him, he heard yelling and laughing. He opened his eyes again. The night sky seemed to be spinning, and in its vortex, he saw Ballantine and Honeycutt. He fixed his vision on the bounty hunter's long blond pigtail. He tried to concentrate, to ignore the pain that was boring inside him. Now the ants were devouring his skin, next they would work their way inside, to his muscles and vital organs. It would take them a while, though. A long while.

Cole had no idea how much time had passed. *Concentrate*, he told himself. *Concentrate. Ignore the pain. Look at Honeycutt's pigtail. Try to count the twists in the braid.* He heard Ballantine laughing; the laughter seemed to come from far away. Honeycutt's blond pigtail swam in his vision. It moved like it was alive, like a snake. Nearby, someone was screaming, and Cole realized that it was him. The Apaches had taught him to endure pain, but he had never felt pain like this. His Apache father, Loco, would have been disappointed. Cole could see the old man's reproving face in front of him, but he didn't care. He screamed. He cried out. He fought the ropes that held him down. *Father, I'm sorry. I'm not worthy. I'm sorry.*

Above his screams, he heard something else. Gunshots. Then more of them.

"Apaches!" someone cried. "The Apaches have come! Get back to the mission!"

There was a great upheaval around Cole. People struggled to their feet. They dropped bottles of tequila and ran for the safety of the promontory and the mission. More shots sounded.

"Hurry!" Ballantine cried. "Get back before they cut us off!"

Honeycutt pointed to Cole. "What about him?"

"He's not going anywhere," Ballantine told him. "Come on."

The two men followed the others to the mission. The scalp hunters and their women retreated pell mell up the hill. A minute later, out of the darkness, a deeper shadow appeared. The shadow knelt beside Cole. It was a woman.

"Elena," he groaned.

"Yes," she said. She scooped dirt over his chest and neck, more and more of it, smothering the ants, momentarily lessening the pain. She sawed his bonds with a knife.

"You fired those shots," Cole realized.

"Yes. Now, get away, while you can. Go upstream and hide."

Cole sat up, half delirious, rubbing the circulation back into his wrists and legs. The ants were still all over him, imprisoned by molasses and dirt, still biting him. He tried to brush away the sticky mess. It did no good. He felt like he was on fire.

"Come . . . come with me," he croaked to Elena.

"No," she said.

"But Ballantine. He'll . . ."

"No, he won't. In his way, Thomas cares for me. I'll be all right."

She hesitated, and her voice lowered. "Anyway, you . . . you do not really want me. I know that. I would just be an encumbrance to you."

She was right, and Cole hated himself because of it. "Elena, I — "

She put a finger to his lips, cutting him off. "No. Now, go. Quickly. Please."

She helped him to his feet. He tried to brush away the ants again, then gave up. The pain was so great that he couldn't think. He felt like he was going mad.

"Go," she said again, and she gave him a little push. Then she was gone herself, hurrying toward the promontory.

From the mission, there were rifle shots. Some fools up there had gotten jumpy and opened fire at nothing. All the more luck for Cole. He stumbled along, hoping he was headed in the direction of the river. How long he walked, he didn't know. He didn't even know if he was going in a straight line. Pain consumed him. Several times he fell to the ground and rolled in the dirt like a dog or a bear, trying to scrape off the ants. Then he got back up again and kept going.

At last his moccasined feet splashed water. The river. He cried with relief and waded to the middle of the stream. He let the cold water come up his body, over his waist, over his chest, up to his neck. He felt the pain recede. Then the ants were climbing for safety, hundreds of them, up his neck and jaws, into his nose, his hair. He let himself slip under water. He stayed down as long as he could. He got up, took a deep breath, and went under again, washing the ants from his body and out of his hair. He stayed down until he thought his lungs would explode, then he raised his head. He went under one more time, then dragged himself to the far side of the stream. Thank God it wasn't deep; he couldn't have swum.

He reached the far shore. He lay there and took a drink. Then he crept along the shore, digging up mud. He packed the mud onto his chest and ribs and as much of his back as he could reach. He packed it around his neck, over his face and in his hair, to soothe the pain. Then he crawled downstream as far as he could go. It wasn't as far as he would have liked, but it couldn't be helped. If the scalp hunters searched for him tomorrow, they were bound to find him. He had to hope they rode out at first light, like Ballantine had planned.

He found a stand of brush. He pushed himself into its cover, heedless of the thorns that scratched him, and he fell asleep. His sleep was broken by waves of pain, and in his tormented dreams he heard screaming.

Chapter 20

Cole came to. Flies buzzed dully in his mud-caked ears. He could tell by the light that filtered through the brush that it was midday. What had seemed like good cover last night was hardly anything at all when viewed by day. He would have been plainly visible to anyone riding by. The scalp hunters must not have looked for him. They must have deserted their base at first light, as they had planned to do, scared of Nanay and his Apaches.

Cole tried to get up, but a wave of pain and nausea forced him back down. His neck was stiff and raw from being dragged by the rope, and it was hard to move his head. He remembered the ant hills, the feeling as the tiny creatures swarmed over him, devouring him. The mud on his body had dried stiff and heavy, like a plaster cast. Beneath it, his skin was raw and excruciatingly painful.

He had a burning thirst. He heard water gurgling and knew that he must be near the stream. Slowly, painfully, he rolled onto his stomach. He lay there a second, catching his breath, while the pain receded. He dragged himself forward, thorns cutting his skin in the places it was not protected by the mud, and he stuck his head from the brush.

He watched and listened. There seemed to be no one about. Birds were singing. Across the stream, about a half-mile distant, he saw vultures swooping low behind a dip in the hill. They must be feeding on a dead horse or mule, abandoned by the scalp hunters in their flight.

Cole crawled to the stream, pulling himself along, still watchful, trying to ignore the pain that consumed him. Even his teeth hurt. He was out of breath and sweating under the mud pack when he reached the water. He lay and drank.

He could see the promontory clearly from here. It looked quiet. The corn fields and cattle in the little valley were unattended, more evidence that Ballantine and his scalp hunters had pulled out.

Should he try to catch them? He had no horse, no weapons. He hated to let Ballantine do this to him and get away with it, but maybe he should leave well enough alone, and be thankful that he was still alive. It was only because of Elena that he *was* alive. He hoped she was all right.

He drank some more. The water revived him. He realized that he was famished. If he had the time, he could make a bow and arrows and kill one of the steers that grazed in the valley. But there was no time. The Apaches might appear at any moment, and when they did, they weren't likely to be in a good mood.

The best place to find food would be on the promontory. Surely, in their flight, the scalp hunters and their camp followers had left something behind. He might find weapons up there, as well, maybe even a horse.

When Cole had finished drinking, he stripped off his trousers and moccasins, and he bathed himself in the river, washing the mud from his skin and hair. His skin was red and raw; it oozed blood from the attacks of the ants. Exposure to the air was painful, and the slightest movement made it worse. Cole grit his teeth. Tears flowed down his scarred cheek. He covered his chest, arms, and neck with a thinner layer of mud. The mud would take the edge off the pain, and it would cool him against the heat.

Slowly, he put his pants and moccasins back on. He crossed the stream. He was still watchful, but there was no movement, no sign of human life. He seemed to be alone in the valley. What if he was wrong? What if some of the scalp hunters were still up there, watching him even now? Common sense told him that was not likely, however, not with Nanay on their trail.

He left the stream and crossed the ground he had traversed the night before. It all seemed different. He felt pain with each step. Now and then the delirium of last night threatened to return, and he had to stop. He was weak, and breath came with difficulty.

He started up the hill toward the promontory. Ahead, he saw the vultures. Then he topped the little rise in the hill, and he stopped.

In front of him was a body, or something that had once been a body, because most of it was now bones and raw meat. It was staked out on the row of ant hills, where Cole himself had been. The ants still crowded on it, making it seem like it was quivering, and now the vultures had joined in.

Cole stumbled forward, yelling, throwing rocks at the hideous birds. "Get away! Go!"

The vultures flapped their long wings, reluctant to leave their feed."Go! God damn it, go!" Cole cried, hurling rocks wildly at them, unable to aim because of the tears in his eyes. At last, the vultures lifted slowly and awkwardly from the ground. They circled overhead, as Cole ran forward to the body.

"Oh, God," he said.

It was Elena.

Cole fell to his knees and hung his head.

Ballantine had staked Elena to the ant hills as punishment for her saving Cole's life. The screams that Cole had heard last night had been no dream. They had been Elena's. A hole in the girl's skull showed that, at some point, someone had mercifully put an end to her agony. In his deep sleep, Cole hadn't heard the shot.

Cole turned away. Elena had loved him, or thought that she did. She'd been with these depraved scalp hunters for so long that a man like Cole had seemed virtuous to her. She had thought she'd seen good qualities in Cole, qualities she had only imagined. She had realized that Cole had no feelings for her, though; so rather than be a burden, she had not come with him. She had trusted in Ballantine's affection for her, and that trust had cost her life.

Cole was shaking with rage and self-hatred. It was his fault that this had happened. If he had killed Ballantine when he had the chance, Elena would still be alive. He had let his humanity — his sense of friendship — overcome his reason.

He would not make that mistake again, as long as he lived.

Cole's jaw was clenched so tight that it hurt. He was going after Ballantine and his men. He was going to catch them, however long it took, whatever obstacles he might have to overcome. And this time when he caught them, he was not going to hesitate. He was going to kill them. And he was going to enjoy doing it.

He cut Elena's body — it wasn't really a body, any more — free. He dragged it into the shade and piled heavy rocks on top of it. He could at least keep the birds and wild animals off her. There was no time for anything more elaborate. He would have said a prayer over her, but he was not a praying man. Not anymore. Torn between the white man's God and the gods of the Apaches, he had found solace in none.

Now it was time for revenge.

He started back to the promontory, moving warily from cover to cover, where there was any. He came across fresh tracks where the scalp hunters had departed that morning. Not far from where he had buried Elena, the tracks split. A large group of horses and mules had gone downstream, toward Mexico. That looked to be the women and the few men who serviced the scalp hunters on the promontory — the cantina owner, and some others. Four sets of prints broke off from the main body and crossed the stream, heading toward the *Jornada*, and the States. Cole recognized the prints of Ballantine's horse among them.

There were the prints of one horse that Cole didn't see — the ones belonging to Honeycutt, the huge bounty hunter. Cole backtracked, but he found nothing. A man that size, his horse's prints would be impossible to miss. He hadn't gone with the women, or with Ballantine.

Which meant — what? Had Honeycutt been killed by Ballantine and his men? Could be. They didn't trust Honeycutt. For all Honeycutt's talk about having no quarrel with the scalp hunters, Ballantine and his men were worth more money dead than Cole was, and money was one hell of a motivator.

So Honeycutt was dead, or else he was out there somewhere, looking for Cole, willing to chance being caught by the Apaches, in return for possession of Cole's head.

Cole reached the causeway that led onto the promontory. He lay there a while, watching. The old mission seemed quiet. Even at this distance, Cole could see evidence of the scalp hunters' hasty departure. Lying in the brush, Cole was so weak and hungry that he almost fell asleep. He fought the urge to give in to his weariness and pain. He pushed himself to keep going.

He got to his feet and crossed the causeway. The rock fell away steeply on either side of him. He passed through the mission gate and across the yard. He passed the church. The ground was littered with discarded articles of clothing, with bottles and old carpet bags. Even the chickens and goats were gone.

Beyond the church, Cole came to a string of adobe shacks and brush *jacales*. The adobe buildings looked slightly more substantial than the *jacales*, so he decided to try them first. He approached the first one, pushed aside the cow hide that served as a door and stepped inside.

It was dark in here, and cool. On a crude table in the center of the front room was a stack of tortillas. *Jackpot*, he thought. He crammed the stale tortillas in his mouth; he'd eaten a lot worse when he was on the trail with Loco. There was an *olla*, a clay water jug, nearby. Cole unstopped it and smelled. Mescal. His stomach turned, and he tossed the jug across the room. Another *olla* contained water, and he used it to wash down the tortillas. He searched the house for more substantial food, but there was nothing. There were no weapons, either, save for a *cuchillo*, a long, thin-bladed Mexican knife that Cole stuck in his belt.

Cole pushed aside the cow hide flap, starting for the next house. As he did, there was a shot, and a bullet plowed into the adobe next to his head.

Chapter 21

Cole dropped back inside the adobe house, breathing hard. A second shot chipped the door jamb, spraying him with adobe dust.

It was dark in here, with the cow hide filling the door and the small rear window closed. "You had ten minutes to set up that shot, Honeycutt," Cole called out. "Is that the best you can do?"

The pigtailed bounty hunter was in the doorway of the house opposite. He called back in his gruff voice. "You son of a bitch. If you hadn't broke my glasses, I'd of put that bullet between your eyes."

Cole sat with his back to the wall. "You should carry an extra pair."

"I do. They got broke when you shot my horse from under me."

Cole had to laugh. The laughter made his entire body ache. He felt fresh blood oozing beneath the layer of mud with which he'd covered himself. Honeycutt must have stalked him across the mission yard, yet Cole hadn't been aware of his presence. Cole had to admit that Honeycutt was good. The big man must be unsure whether Cole had a gun. That's why he didn't come right after him.

"How come you waited for me here?" Cole yelled.

"Figured you had to come back," Honeycutt said. "Why go looking for you and maybe miss you, or even walk into some kind of trap?"

"You're either clever or lazy, Honeycutt. I ain't figured out which."

That got Honeycutt mad. He said, "Figure this out, asshole." He left the doorway and started toward the adobe house.

There was no back way out of here. Cole's only hope lay with Honeycutt's bad eyes. Cole gathered himself. He thrust aside the cow hide, dashed out the door, and dived across the ground, rolling.

Honeycutt snapped a shot at him but missed. Cole came to his feet. The dive and roll had torn his ravaged upper body open. The pain almost took his breath away. He got his legs under him and ran around the side of the house as another bullet thwacked into the adobe behind him.

Honeycutt swore and came after him. Cole moved behind the house, putting another wall between himself and the bounty hunter's rifle. He had to outrun Honeycutt. He had to get off the promontory and into the mountains, where he could hide.

He moved to the rear of the next house and stopped, catching his breath. His body wanted to quit, but he had to make it keep going. He wondered if Honeycutt had gotten a fresh horse from the scalp hunters, and if he had, where it was.

Behind him there was no sound. Honeycutt had stopped again, waiting for Cole to make the next move.

Looking around, Cole realized that he had moved in the opposite direction from the mission gate. He was farther from leaving the promontory than ever. He could climb down the promontory's steep rock sides, but it would be a slow climb, and he would make a great target that way — even for somebody with bad eyes, like Honeycutt. A climb like that would take time, too. If Honeycutt had a horse, he could ride around and wait for Cole at the bottom. Cole had no weapon to fight the bounty hunter except the *cuchillo* he'd found in the house. He couldn't match Honeycutt physically — he'd already learned that.

He'd have to try and work his way along these houses, past the stables, past the church, and out the gate. Maybe he could catch Honeycutt looking the other way.

Where *was* Honeycutt, anyway? The big bastard was silent as a cat. It was hard to believe. Cole's senses were alive. The hair on his forearms was standing up. He smelled Honeycutt. The bounty hunter was close, but that was all Cole knew.

Cole wiped sweat from his eyes. His body was in agony after diving along the rocky ground, but he had to put the pain out of his mind. Before him was a little warren of adobe houses and brush *jacales*. Cole drew in his breath. He set himself. He ran to his left and turned down the side of a *jacale*.

And found Honeycutt right in front of him.

Cole threw himself to the ground as Honeycutt's rifle went off. Cole heard the bullet whine overhead. He got up and scrambled back around the side of the *jacale*. He ran down the narrow lane for all he was worth, turned right, and headed for the stables. Honeycutt's footsteps were right behind him. On top of everything else, the bastard was fast. The rifle fired again. Splinters flew from a *jacale*'s brush wall.

Cole broke into the open, running past what had once been the mission granary. He stumbled in an old wagon rut, fell to one hand, got up and kept going. He saw the mission gate in the distance, but he didn't have the strength left to get there. In his condition he couldn't outrun Honeycutt anyway. He dodged right, in front of the old mission church. He ducked inside the carved church doorway, tripping in the dirt and trash that covered the flagstone floor.

He got up. It was gloomy inside the church. Sunbeams filtered through the windows and the partly collapsed roof. In front of him were the dusty, littered altar and the wooden *reredos*, or screen, behind it. The faded native frescoes stared down from the walls. Cole shivered. The place seemed full of ghosts. Tethered to a stone candle holder in the far wall was a horse — Honeycutt's.

Behind Cole it was quiet again. Honeycutt must be waiting to see if Cole tried to sneak through the church and out the back door that led from the sacristy. Cole looked around, then padded through the narrow door that led to the bell tower.

The tower's cupola roof was still intact. Light came through the windows just below it. A wooden landing ran around the bell floor. The two floors in between had collapsed or been cannibalized for their wood, but Cole saw hand holds chiseled into the tower's wall.

He began to climb.

He moved as fast as he could. He would hide in the shadows on the bell floor. With luck, Honeycutt would think he had somehow gotten out of the church unnoticed. He would go looking for Cole off the promontory. By the time he realized his mistake and came back, Cole would be long gone.

Cole reached the bell floor. The ancient boards creaked as he tested their weight. He stepped into what looked like the darkest corner. The floor collapsed beneath him. He jumped back, crouching against the fieldstone wall as the broken floor boards fell the length of the tower to the well below, where they landed with a crash. Honeycutt was bound to hear that.

Cole looked around. An old ladder was propped against the wall. It just reached the crossbeam which supported the bronze bell. That gave Cole an idea.

He began climbing the ladder. He didn't have much time. Near the top, one of the ancient rungs gave way beneath his feet. He slipped and almost fell off. Then he steadied himself, pulled himself up to the next rung, and began to climb again.

He reached the heavy crossbeam. He swung onto it, his injured body groaning with pain. He crawled along the crossbeam. He prayed that the beam would hold his weight along with the weight of the hundred-pound bell. If it didn't, it was a long drop.

He got to the bell. The bronze had turned green from age and lack of polishing. There were three loops at the bell's top — representing the Trinity, Cole guessed. Heavy chains had been passed through each of these loops, then bolted around the crossbeam. As Cole had hoped, the iron chains were rusted through. Cole drew the *cuchillo* from his belt. He worked the knife blade into the bolt closure. The rusted metal flaked away. Cole dug at the metal. More fell away. He kept digging, sawing through the rust. Then he was through. The chain was broken. Noiselessly, he drew the chain from the bronze loop and hung it over the crossbeam. He began to work on the next chain.

Below, he heard Honeycutt enter the church. The big bounty hunter must have heard the floor boards falling. He must know that Cole had not tried to get out the back way. Cole heard faint footfalls on the stone floor.

"Taggart?" It was Honeycutt's voice.

Cole kept cutting through the second chain. Sweat poured into his eyes. He wiped them on his shoulder. Waves of pain swept over him until he thought he would faint, but he fought through them.

The footsteps withdrew to the far end of the church, toward the wooden *reredos*.

There — Cole broke second chain. Quietly, he withdrew it from the bell's loop and frantically started working on the last, center chain.

The footsteps were coming closer again. Cole was almost through the center bolt. Putting the *cuchillo* aside, he lay on the crossbeam and took the hundred-pound bell's other two loops in his hands. Gently, he let the bell down, until its weight snapped what was left of the bolt. The chain fell to the floor below with a thunk.

Honeycutt heard the noise. He approached the bell tower. "Taggart?"

"In here," Cole said, grimacing. The veins on his arms and neck stood out as he lay astride the crossbeam, holding the great bell.

Honeycutt was confident. "You're hit, ain't you?"

"Yeah." Cole didn't have to fake the strain in his voice. His arm and shoulder muscles were shaking.

Far below, Honeycutt's bulk filled the ill-lit tower well. The bounty hunter was puzzled as he looked around. "Where the hell are you?"

Cole let go of the heavy bell. He watched it fall through space. "Here," he said.

Honeycutt looked up. For a second, the expression on his myopic face froze. Then the bell hit his head with a crunch and a doleful gong.

Chapter 22

Cole swung off the crossbeam, onto the ladder. He climbed slowly down the bell tower. Honeycutt was dead, but there had never been any doubt about that. The pigtailed bounty hunter's skull had been crushed by the falling bell. From beneath the bell, blood and brains spilled across the stone floor.

Cole took the dead man's rifle, pistol, and shell belt. With an effort, he removed Honeycutt's shirt from the heavy body, trying not to look at the bounty hunter's smashed head. He put on the shirt for protection from the sun. The shirt was huge on him, so he sliced off the sleeves with his *cuchillo*.

He stumbled outside the bell tower, crossing the mission yard to the well. He winched up the bucket and drank. He splashed water on his face. He was tired and feverish. He would have given anything to lie down and sleep, but that was not an option. The Apaches could come at any time, and Ballantine and his men already had at least an eight-hour start on him.

He went back inside the church, where he searched Honeycutt's saddlebags. He found plug tobacco, jerky, and tortillas — Honeycutt's provisions for crossing the *Jornada*. There were four canteens full of water, plus grain for the horse. Cole rolled a piece of the jerky in one of the tortillas and wolfed it down. He threw away the things that he would not need, like the tobacco, then he saddled and bridled the bounty hunter's big gray gelding.

He mounted and rode away from the mission. The horse was adequate at best. It had bottom, but not much speed. With its size, it would use up a lot of water and grain. It was not the mount that Cole would have picked to catch Ballantine in the *Jornada* — he would have preferred his old sorrel gelding, or a mule. The gray would have to do, though.

Cole rode down from the hills, into the little valley. Near the stream, he paused. With Honeycutt's rifle, he shot one of the scalp hunters' abandoned steers. He cut out the animal's liver and ate the salty organ raw, a delicacy to which he'd become accustomed in his days with the Apaches. He cut strips of meat for later. But he hadn't killed the steer primarily for food. He emptied the animal's intestine, rinsing it thoroughly in the stream. He tied the intestine at one end with a strip of rawhide. He filled it with water from the stream, then tied off the other end. He made a rope sling and hung the water-filled intestine from his saddle horn, to go with Honeycutt's canteens.

He rode on, following the scalp hunters' trail. They were leaving by the same route that Cole and Ballantine had used to come in. They would probably cross the *Jornada* by the same route, as well. Cole picked up his pace, pausing only now and then to be sure he was still on their trail. He climbed high into the Eagle Mountains, into the land of pines and crisp air.

That night, he camped among the pines. It was cold, but he dared not risk a fire. He was used to freezing nights like this, without fire, from days spent roaming the mountains with the Apaches, hiding from American and Mexican soldiers. He ate some of the beef strips that he had cut that afternoon, along with Honeycutt's tortillas. He grained the big gray gelding and set him to graze.

Cole slept fitfully that night. He was in too much pain to be comfortable. The next day, he was off well before dawn. Early that morning he crossed the divide and began his descent from the mountains. Before noon, he was on the *Jornada del Fuego*. He figured he'd made up an hour and a half on the fleeing scalp hunters. Their tracks were easy enough to read. Along with Ballantine, there were three others in the group — Slocum, Kingsley, and Werdann, most likely.

Cole pushed the gray gelding hard. He still had six and a half hours to make up. Once again, he fought the spell of the *Jornada*, where time seemed to stand still under the relentless onslaught of the sun. He had to urge both himself and the gelding on. He was feverish from being staked out on the ant hills. He drifted in and out of consciousness, awakening once with a start to find that his horse had stopped. He looked at the sun. Nearly an hour had passed. He swore and kicked the horse's ribs savagely. He would need to be in better shape than this when he caught up with Ballantine and his men.

Then he remembered Elena. He remembered what she had looked like when the scalp hunters were done with her. He remembered the Apaches that he had seen slaughtered in the Sierra Negros, and the family of sheepherders. The fog seemed to lift from his brain and he recovered his grim sense of purpose.

He rode through the noon heat, sparing neither himself nor his mount. This leg of the journey was different from the one he'd made with Ballantine, due to the detour they'd taken in pursuit of Nanay. He was not sure where the next water was, so he had to stop at sunset. He didn't want to lose the scalp hunters' tracks.

He was off again as soon as it was light enough to read sign. At about eight that morning, he came to a little *tinaja* where Ballantine and his men had stopped the previous evening. The *tinaja* was high in the hills, and there wasn't much water left in it. The signs showed that the scalp hunters had not stayed here, however. There had still been daylight left, so they had ridden on after watering themselves and their animals. Cole watered the gelding, then he topped off his canteens and the steer's intestine with the scummy water, and he kept going. About two hours later, he came to the place where the scalp hunters had camped. Like him, they had made a cold camp. They were fearful of pursuit by Nanay and the Apaches. They didn't know about Cole.

Cole found an empty whiskey bottle at the camp and picked it up. "So Ballantine still has trouble sleeping," he said. He threw the bottle away, breaking it on the rocks. "He should."

Cole remembered this country now. He was confident that Ballantine and his men would make for the box canyon seep spring next. Cole knew the way there. With only the briefest of rests, he traveled the remainder of the day and long into the night, guiding himself by the stars. Tomorrow night the scalp hunters would seek water at the *tinaja* called Dead Man's Tanks.

Cole intended to give that name renewed meaning.

It was well before sunup the next day when Cole broke camp. The gray gelding was holding up better than he had expected. The horse had done everything Cole had asked of him, however reluctantly. Then, in the predawn darkness, the big gray misfooted in a shallow ravine and came up lame.

Cole dismounted. The gray was holding up its right foreleg. A quick examination told Cole that the leg was broken. Cole was alone on the desert, without a horse.

Cole killed the horse, slitting its throat with the *cuchillo*. He could not chance a gunshot. It had been a good horse, and he wished it could have suffered a better fate. He took the jerky and some of the tortillas from the saddlebag and put them in his shirt. He drew the Smith & Wesson hunting rifle from its scabbard. He crammed his shirt and trouser pockets with bullets. He tied his pistol holster down so that it wouldn't slap against his leg. He filled the steer's intestine with water from the canteens, then he drank the rest of the water in the canteens and tossed them away. He slung the intestine over his shoulder. Lastly, he tied his bandana around his head, Apache style, to keep the hair and sweat out of his eyes.

Then he took the rifle in his right hand and he began to run.

Chapter 23

Cole followed the scalp hunters' tracks.

An Apache could travel faster on foot than a white man could on horseback. Cole remembered his Apache foster father, Loco, taking him on long training runs in the mountains, to build up his wind and legs. Cole had been proud of his ability to run, once. He had prided himself on being as good as any Apache. But it had been a long time since those training runs, and Loco hadn't staked him on an ant hill first.

It took a while for Cole to get his legs under him. He wasn't used to this anymore. His breath came hard. The sweat made the wounds on his body burn. In addition, all the water he'd drunk before he had started lay heavy in his stomach. That was all right, though — he'd use up that water, and more, before he was through.

Gradually, his breathing became more regular. His legs stopped feeling like blocks of wood. They grew stronger, more supple. He began to get a rhythm. His body began to feel like that of an animal, operating smoothly and efficiently. He jogged along, taking short steps, with no wasted motion of arms or head. When the rifle grew heavy, he switched it to his other hand. Now and then he stopped to sip from the intestine full of water, then he kept going.

The sun rose higher. The fierce heat beat down. The sweat dried as it came out of Cole's body, leaving only the salt to burn his wounds. Once again, he passed the detritus of westward expansion — wagons, graves, abandoned furniture and equipment. The country was rugged, ridge after ridge of barren, rocky hills, whose mineral content made them look purple when seen from a distance. There were no trees, no mesquite, no cactus. Here and there a forlorn clump of creosote stood out, the only living things on this sun-baked eternity of sand and rock.

Hell must look something like this, Cole thought.

The rocks absorbed the sun's heat and reflected it back in shimmering waves. It was like running in an oven, but Cole kept on, through the morning and into the afternoon. He was gaining on the scalp hunters; he could tell from their tracks. He was not that far behind them now.

He had to plan what to do when he caught them. Ideally, he would get to Dead Man's Tanks before they did. If he controlled the water, he could force them to come to him. They'd have no choice, if they didn't want to die of thirst. It would be hard to get to the tanks before Ballantine and his men did, though, since he would have to make a long detour to avoid being seen. His other choice was to let the scalp hunters get there first and make camp. Cole could hit them late at night. With luck, he'd catch Ballantine drunk, maybe all of them. Or, he could attack them at dawn and hope that Ballantine and his men were too surprised or too hung over to put up much resistance.

It was mid-afternoon. The harsh shadows were beginning to lengthen. Cole topped another long, rock-strewn ridge. Then he stopped.

Something moved in the distance.

It was a rider.

Cole crouched low on the skyline, shading his eyes with a hand. The rider was white — Cole could tell by the way he sat his horse. It was one of the scalp hunters; Cole couldn't recognize him at this range. The man had straggled behind the others. Maybe he'd had problems with his horse, or maybe the scalp hunters were losing discipline in their flight — though that was hard to believe with Ballantine in charge.

Cole examined the landscape. He didn't want any shooting, if possible. He looked for a place where he could intercept the rider. The man was following a natural trail through the rocky country. Farther ahead, Cole saw a narrow pass. If the man kept his present course — as he was almost bound to do — he would go that way.

Cole dropped back below the ridge and ran to his right. He would circle around the rider, get ahead of him, and cut him off. He moved easily along the uneven ground, hopping from rock to rock where he had to. His blood lust was up, and all the pain he had endured seemed to fall away.

He got far out to the right, then turned and began to run parallel to the rider, keeping a long, irregular ridge between them. A lizard skittered out of his way.

The man had not been riding fast. When Cole thought he was well in front of him, he moved cautiously to the top of the ridge to check. He lay among the rocks of the ridge line, blending in, ignoring their red-hot surfaces as best he could. The rider was a good mile behind, coming on at a slow walk, every now and then looking behind him. Cole looked in the other direction. There was no sign of the other scalp hunters.

Cole moved on, to the spot where the trail narrowed. He hastened down from the ridge. The pass took a bend just before this, so Cole was in no danger of being seen by the rider. When he reached the valley floor, he took off his shirt and tied it around his waist, as an Apache did when preparing for battle. He hid his rifle, shell belt, food, and water skin in the rocks. He wouldn't be needing them. He rubbed dirt in his hair. He rubbed dirt over his ravaged body, grimacing with the pain that action caused. He rubbed dirt into his trousers. Then he drew the long Mexican *cuchillo* from his belt. He lay beside the trail, and he threw more dirt over himself, until he was completely covered. He grasped the *cuchillo* in his right hand.

He lay motionless under the beating sun. He stared straight ahead, willing himself to become a part of the landscape, the way Loco had taught him, long ago.

He smelled the horse and the man, smelled their rank sweat. Then he heard the steady *clop-clop* of hoofs.

Closer they came. Cole did not move, not even his eyes. The rider would suspect nothing. If he was looking anywhere for trouble, it would be up in the rocks.

Closer. Cole's hand tightened on the *cuchillo*'s wooden grip. He gathered his muscles beneath him, ready to spring.

Closer. Man and horse were alongside him now, not five feet away.

Cole jumped from the ground. A bounding step took him to the horse, and he leaped with the knife poised. He saw that the rider was Kingsley — he recognized him from the bandage around his head — even as he tackled him and slit his throat.

Both men toppled off the horse's opposite side, landing in the dirt. The scalp hunter scrabbled on his back, like a dying insect. He grasped at his throat, with the blood spurting out of him and the life fading from his eyes. Then his legs kicked out once, and he was still.

Kingsley's frightened horse had run off down the trail. *Let him go*, Cole thought. He was doing better on foot. Maybe the Apaches would catch the poor beast before the coyotes did — though it was hard to say which group would treat the animal worse.

Cole wiped the bloody knife blade on his pants leg. He looked at the dead scalp hunter. For a moment he felt sorry for Kingsley. Then he remembered how Kingsley had shotgunned the Apache child during the attack on the village. He remembered how Kingsley had laughed when he'd spread the molasses over Cole's chest, by the ant hills, and he wondered if Kingsley had poured the molasses on Elena, as well.

Cole's expression hardened. His only regret was that the bastard never knew who had done this to him.

Cole got his water skin and took a drink. He buckled on his shell belt. He picked up his rifle and started running again.

Chapter 24

Slocum and Werdann stood beside their horses. The blazing afternoon sun beat down on them; there was no shade on the vast expanse of the *Jornada*. Werdann held the reins of Ballantine's mount, as well as his own. Above them, Ballantine stood at the crest of a ridge, looking over their back trail. Slocum and Werdann were hot and tired. They were low on water, and it showed in their dusty, sunburned faces. The gaunted horses hung their heads low, as if in submission to the relentless assault of the sun.

"Christ, I hate this country," Slocum said. The sun had dried the grease from his face, leaving only the dirt. It seemed to have melted his jowls, which hung limp.

Werdann, the rawhide lean Texan, agreed. "When I get out of here, I want to go someplace where it rains — or snows, even. I almost wish we'd took our chances and gone back through the mountains to Hermosillo. Least that way if we died, we'd have been looking at something green. Ain't nothin' out here but rocks. Ain't nothin' *alive*."

There was a little shower of stones as Ballantine descended the ridge, a worried look on his face. He blinked his eyes against the sun's harsh glare and the headache that last night's bottle of whiskey had given him. It seemed like he always had a headache, anymore.

Slocum said, "You see Kingsley, Colonel?"

Ballantine shook his head. "No sign of him. And you can see damn far from up there."

Slocum and Werdann exchanged glances. "Kingsley wasn't that far behind us," Slocum said. "What do you think happened to him?"

"I think he's dead," Ballantine told them.

Ballantine lifted his canteen from his saddle. He shook it to see how much water was left. Not much. He unscrewed the cap and took a drink. "I warned him to be careful when he started falling behind with that damn horse of his."

Slocum said, "That's Kingsley for you. He never did know how to take care of no horse."

Neither Slocum nor Werdann missed Kingsley. Kingsley had been a small-time criminal and saloon fighter, a bully who thought with his fists.

Werdann shifted uneasily. His tight, thin-soled cowman's boots hurt his feet when there was a lot of walking to be done, as there had been today. "You figure Apaches got him?"

"Or Honeycutt," Ballantine said.

"Honeycutt!" said Werdann.

Ballantine took another drink, then replaced the canteen on his saddle horn. "I've been expecting Honeycutt to come after us. I just didn't think he could catch us this soon."

"But why?" Werdann persisted. "Honeycutt's the one that put us on to Taggart."

"Why do you think?" Ballantine asked. "Money. A fellow like Honeycutt may say that all he wants to do is kill Taggart and collect the reward on him, but sooner or later he's going to start thinking about dollars. He's a bounty hunter, and we're bounty."

Slocum said, "I expect it wouldn't hurt his reputation none if he kills him the leader of the scalp hunters."

Ballantine nodded. "Precisely. So either we finish him off now, or we spend the rest of this trip looking over our shoulders for him. To tell the truth, I've been planning for this. I intended to wait for Honeycutt at that cantina at the end of the *Jornada* and kill him there." He grinned at his companions. "You see, even if he wasn't after us, he'll be carrying Taggart's head. That's what that Higgins fellow in Lincoln County wanted as proof. We'll relieve Honeycutt of the head and give it to Higgins ourselves. That's fifteen hundred dollars in addition to what we'll get for these scalps. Enough to keep us going for a while."

Werdann said, "You sure he'll have Taggart's head?"

"He'll have it. Fat fool showed me the jar he meant to stick it in."

"I mean, are you sure he was able to find Taggart and kill him?"

Slocum answered before Ballantine could. "Jesus, Werdann. You saw Taggart. He was more dead than alive when we left him on them ant hills. He couldn't have gone very far. He couldn't have took on a five-year-old in his condition, much less somebody like that big bastard Honeycutt."

Werdann said, "Still hard to believe it's Honeycutt after us, not with that beat-up horse we give him."

Slocum bit off a fingernail with his bad teeth. He spit out the nail and the dirt that had come with it. "Maybe he got another horse, somehow. He was capable of anything."

Werdann sneered. "You sound like you're scared of him."

"Shut up, Werdann. You think 'cause you was a hired gun for them Texas ranchers, you're some kind of hot shit. You think you're better'n anybody else in the outfit."

"Maybe I do," Werdann admitted. He had ridden for some of the big Texas cattle spreads in their feuds with incoming farmers and with each other. When the law had come in, and work had gotten scarce, he'd drifted west. He said, "What I did, it was like a profession. It was honorable, kind of. We had us a code."

Slocum scoffed. "Shootin' grangers in the back? Some code."

"At least I only done men, and most of them was looking to do me first. I didn't kill no women. I didn't kill my wife. I didn't kill that whore in Denver and chop her into pieces."

Slocum's heavy lower lip trembled. Back in Ohio, Slocum had been a freight driver. One night, in a fit of drunken jealousy, he had killed his unfaithful wife. Worse, he had found that he enjoyed doing it. He had fled west, where he had become a bar bouncer and loan collector. Then he'd gotten drunk again and killed a prostitute in Denver. He'd enjoyed that, too, especially cutting her up. Western society didn't pay much attention to the murder of prostitutes, but it objected to mutilation, so Slocum had fled to Santa Fe, one step ahead of Judge Lynch. There, he'd met Ballantine and joined the scalp hunters.

To Werdann, Slocum retorted, "I notice your fancy code don't stop you from killing Apache women, or their kids."

"All right," Werdann amended, "I don't kill *white* women. It ain't like Injuns is real people, after all. Hell, even niggers is more like people than Injuns." He sniffed. "Anyway, when I kill Injuns, or anybody else, it's business. I do it for money. You do it 'cause you like it. You ain't right in the head, Slocum."

Before Slocum could reply, Ballantine said, "Stop squabbling, you two, and let me think. You're like a couple of schoolboys — not that either of you ever went to school." He took his horse's reins from Werdann. "Come on, let's get moving."

The three men mounted their horses. The leather bag full of Apache scalps still hung from Ballantine's saddle horn.

As they started off, Ballantine theorized aloud. "Somebody's following us, we know that. It's either Apaches or Honeycutt." He looked back. "I wish I had Cole Taggart's nose. He could smell the bastards and tell you who they were."

"That's a damn Injun trick," Slocum said.

Werdann said, " Taggart was part Injun, what I heard."

"Well, now he's all dead," Slocum said. "Serves him right, too, what he done to us — what he done to Quirt Evans. Me and Quirt was pals."

"That don't surprise me," Werdann said in a voice tinged with disgust.

Slocum bristled. "What the hell you mean by that?"

"Enough, I said!" Ballantine told them. "Why don't we just kill each other, and make it easier for whoever's back there?"

In his mind's eye Ballantine pictured the country between here and Dead Man's Tanks, and after that, to Ignacio Cruz's cantina. "Whoever it is, we're going to prepare a little surprise for him."

Slocum said, "You said before we was going to take him out at that cantina."

"I changed my mind. I didn't expect him to catch up to us this fast. I thought we'd have time to get to the cantina and wait for him. After Dead Man's Tanks, the land flattens out. I'd rather ambush him in the hills than have him catch us out on the flats. I want to make sure the initiative stays with us."

Werdann said, "What if it ain't Honeycutt after us? What if it's Apaches?"

"My sixth sense tells me it's Honeycutt," Ballantine said. "But even if it isn't, that doesn't change the plan."

"Which is?"

"We'll fort up at the Tanks. We can wait there a long time. Whoever's after us can't. Eventually they'll have to come for water. Then they'll be ours. You've been to the Tanks, you remember the trail? It winds up that steep canyon. About three-quarters of the way down the canyon, there's a bench where you can look out over the approaches and see, hell, it must be forty miles. Nobody can get near the place without our knowing about it. And when they come . . ." He drew a thumb across his throat.

"Can't they get at us from behind?" Slocum said.

Ballantine shook his head, smiling like the cat that found the cream. "There's a sheer cliff. They come at us from the front, or not at all. I want to get to the Tanks before dark. We'll take care of the horses and get water for ourselves, then we'll set up our little reception. Honeycutt's done a hell of a job to catch up to us like this, but I'm afraid that all it's going to get him is an early grave. Mr. Honeycutt isn't quite as clever as he thinks he is."

Ballantine's smile turned into a grin, then he laughed out loud. The three scalp hunters rode on.

Chapter 25

The mountain in whose canyon recesses lay the *tinaja* known as Dead Man's Tanks rose from the desert like an *Arabian Nights* fortress. Fantastically carved pinnacles and crenellations of rock reached high into the sky. The canyon wound into this stronghold through a wide opening in the mountain's southwestern side. Supposedly, this opening was the only way a man might enter. On this particular night, however, an astute observer might have spied a lone figure climbing the mountain's eastern wall.

Cole Taggart had remembered the canyon entrance to the Tanks. He was afraid that the scalp hunters might be on the lookout for Kingsley, or for whoever had caused Kingsley to disappear. Cole had decided to come to the Tanks by a way the scalp hunters wouldn't expect. He had decided to come the Apache way.

He had started his climb in the late afternoon. By nightfall, he was only halfway to the top. His shirt was still tied around his waist. His rifle was slung across his back, along with the water skin. He had need of both his hands. He could not go as fast as he might have liked, because he was still feverish from his ordeal on the ant hill and tired from the long chase across the *Jornada*. He followed fissures and crevices in the dark, feeling his way. The faint moonlight was some help, but not much. He wanted to be over the top and near the Tanks before dawn. Then he would move on the scalp hunters.

In places, the rock was nearly vertical. Cole had to scale it, feeling for handholds and footholds, at times hanging on by his fingertips and toes. He was only too conscious that a misplaced hand or foot could send him plummeting to the talus below. He pictured himself bouncing off the rocks like a rag doll, the way Paulsen had, when he and his horse had fallen from the rock ledge during the retreat from the Apache village. He remembered the terrified look in Paulsen's eyes just before he fell; he remembered Paulsen's screams. He tried to get all that out of his mind and concentrate on what he was doing. He was an Apache. An Apache could climb anything.

He left the rock wall and picked his way along a boulder-strewn incline. There was a cool breeze up here, far above the desert floor. Above him, a tall pinnacle of rock was silhouetted against the stars. Flat rocks were laid across the pinnacle's top, like a giant table. Cole wondered what strange processes of wind and water had sculpted such a formation.

As Cole neared the pinnacle, he had to scramble up an immense slab of rock. Suddenly the breeze swirled all around his sweaty body, and he knew he had reached the top.

He tried to get his bearings, to figure out where he was in relation to the Tanks. It was difficult to tell in the dark. He'd planned it so that he could go over the top and then straight down, but he'd been forced to angle sideways during the climb, and he wasn't sure where he had ended up. The table-top pinnacle hadn't been visible from the spot on the desert floor where he'd begun his ascent.

He swore. He hadn't planned on taking so long to get to the top. If, after all this, he missed Ballantine and the other two; if by the time he got to the Tanks, they'd broken camp and ridden out . . .

He swore again. He'd never catch them in that case. He was stiff and sore from the climb. He was exhausted from running all day. He'd never be able to put forth that kind of effort again. He should have waited for darkness and gone up the canyon, he thought. He should have taken his chances and hoped the scalp hunters weren't waiting there.

He drank from his water skin, then began working his way down the mountain. The going was almost as steep on this side of the mountain, though there were no more vertical drops.

As he moved through the rock, the land began to take a definite slope to his right. The canyon must be that way. The Tanks were near the canyon's head.

He followed the slope of the land, taking pains to be quiet. He soon found himself in the canyon. He was downwind. Good. The scalp hunters' horses would not pick up his scent.

The short summer night was coming to an end. Cole couldn't see the eastern horizon from here, but he knew that dawn must be breaking, or close to it. He hoped that for once Ballantine and his men hadn't left camp early. He hurried now, unslinging Honeycutt's Smith & Wesson hunting rifle and carrying it in his hand. Was it imagination, or was there a faint lightening of the darkness around him? Yes, it was dawn.

As he neared the canyon bottom, he recognized the landscape from his first trip out here. The Tanks were just ahead. There was the spreading ironwood tree. Cole stopped. The scalp hunters wouldn't be camped right at the Tanks, but a little ways off. Cole bet they'd pick the same place he and Ballantine had used.

Cole cut a wide circle, heading for the campground. Every now and then he stopped to listen. He heard nothing but the song of an early rising cactus wren. He pressed an ear to the ground. There was no faint rumble of hoof beats to tell him that the scalp hunters were riding out of the canyon. Either they had left much earlier, or they were still here.

Then he smelled horses, and a thin smile crossed his lips.

He crept slowly among the rocks. Around him, the dawn had turned everything a flat shade of gray. The air was cool, in contrast to the heat that would soon follow. Cole smelled the fragrant dew, what little of it there was. He smelled the stagnant water in the Tanks.

Then he smelled something else — the remains of a fire. It was the first fire the scalp hunters had built since leaving the old mission. That was odd.

Cole heard the horses now — they were a ways off, stamping their hoofs, blowing. They were picketed in the same draw that he and Ballantine had used before. Good thing they hadn't made this much racket last time.

Cole let the fire's smell guide him to the scalp hunters' campground. Edging around a boulder, he saw the gray remains of the fire. He saw the scalp hunters' saddles and their neatly rolled bedding.

He didn't see the scalp hunters.

A chill ran up Cole's back. He didn't like this. He looked around, half expecting to find them behind him, to find himself trapped. But he was alone.

He watched the camp for a while. He was in no hurry now. The scalp hunters, weren't going anywhere without their horses.

No one appeared.

At last Cole advanced out of the rocks, his finger alongside the hunting rifle's trigger. He knelt by the fire and examined the ashes. From the looks of things, they had built the fire last night — built it good and big, too — then let it burn down. It was like they had wanted to advertise their presence. Why?

Cole moved around the camp. It was easy to pick out the scalp hunters' footprints, three different sets of them. Circling out from the fire, Cole found that the most recent prints led back down the canyon, in a group. He began to have an idea what they might be up to.

Cole went back to the Tanks. He brushed aside the scummy water and took a long drink. He refilled his water skin, then moved down the canyon, following the scalp hunters' footprints. He was alert, quiet. The canyon was just as quiet.

He reached the point where the canyon turned and opened up. The view was panoramic — in the distance, the first rays of the morning sun spread across the desert floor, bathing the high points in soft golden light, while the rest remained in shadow. Already it was getting warmer.

Cole stopped and squatted. He ran his eyes across the broken ground, quartering it.

Then he saw one of them — Slocum. Slocum was crouched in some rocks, scratching himself. Not far away, Cole made out Ballantine, waiting with his rifle. Across the canyon and just above those two was the Texan, Werdann.

They were waiting for Cole, or whoever they thought had caught up to Kingsley. They must know that Kingsley wasn't coming, by now. They must know that they were being pursued, and they must have decided to ambush their pursuer, or pursuers. They were looking down the canyon, watching the entrance.

Slocum shifted in the rocks. He sounded concerned. "Ain't nobody out there, Colonel."

"There will be," Ballantine said confidently. "He'll come. He has to. God himself would eventually have to come to water out here, and this is the only water for thirty miles."

Cole thought about shooting them. No, he'd only be able to get one, then the other two would be alerted. Besides, they were wedged into the rocks so well that hitting them at this distance would be chancy. Better to move in close and take them one by one.

Werdann was the highest up, the closest to him. The Texan sat between two great slabs of rock, watching patiently — but then this probably wasn't the first time he'd taken part in an ambush. He would know how to wait. Cole decided to take him first.

Cole worked down and to his right, along the canyon wall. He moved stealthily, taking care where he put his moccasined feet, lest he knock loose a stone and give away his presence. The sun's rays were creeping over the canyon's far wall, now. The desert below was awash in bright light.

Cole looked away from Werdann as he closed in on him. A man could feel it when someone was staring at his back. The canyon was getting like an oven as hot air rose from the desert floor. Cole ached all over. His upper body was in agony from being staked on the ant hills, and the dirt he'd rubbed all over himself yesterday hadn't made his wounds feel any better.

He was ten yards from Werdann now, above and behind him.

There was a gravelly open space between the two men. Cole stopped. He couldn't get any closer without making noise.

Cole drew the Mexican *cuchillo* from his belt. He balanced it by its long blade. He aimed, drew back his arm, and threw.

The knife sped through the air, turning over once. The blade embedded itself in Werdann's neck, at the base of his skull.

The Texan straightened, grabbing for the knife, trying to pull it out. He stood, almost involuntarily, as if his body were acting independently of his brain. Still trying to pull out the knife, he staggered from between the rocks. Then he toppled onto his face.

There was a shout, followed by a rifle shot. A bullet whined off the rock near Cole's face and he threw himself down.

So much for taking them one by one.

Chapter 26

Cole scrambled into the rocks to get better cover.

Below him, Slocum glimpsed a headband and a bare brown chest. "It ain't Honeycutt," he yelled. "It's an Apache!"

Behind some nearby rocks, Ballantine levered another shell into the chamber of his Winchester. "Christ — no, it's not," he cried back. "It's Taggart!"

"Taggart?" said Slocum. "That's impossible. Taggart's dead."

"Then he has a very active ghost. If you don't believe me, go up and take a closer look. Be careful, though, because he's liable to do to you what he just did to Werdann."

Slocum searched the rugged hillside for sign of their quarry. "How the hell could it be Taggart? And how did he get in here without us seeing him?"

Ballantine said, "Worry about that later. Right now, let's kill him."

Above them, Cole wriggled through the rocks. On the far side of the gravelly open space, he saw Werdann. The Texan was still twitching weakly, the long *cuchillo* sticking out of his neck.

From the other two scalp hunters there was no sound. Cole knew they must be communicating with hand signals. He guessed what they would do. One of them would attempt to pin him down, while the other maneuvered and tried to get a good shot at him. They would try to get him in a cross fire. He poked the hunting rifle through the rocks. He couldn't see either of them.

There was a shot. Cole ducked instinctively. Ballantine's voice sounded, from a different spot than he'd heard it earlier. "Cole — is that really you?"

"It's really me," Cole called back.

"How did you get here?"

"I took the train."

There was another shot. This time Cole fought instinct and didn't duck. He tried to see where the bullet had come from.

"What happened to Honeycutt?" Ballantine said.

"He had a problem with his head," Cole replied.

"His head?"

"He heard bells."

There was a shot from another direction. Cole saw the powder smoke, but he had no target for return fire.

"Did you kill Kingsley?" Ballantine cried.

Cole didn't answer. He couldn't stay here talking. He'd be playing into their hands. He looked around. Above him was a flat-topped rock projection. From that spot, he could cover the lower part of the canyon. He could look down on Slocum and Ballantine.

Cole broke cover and ran for the base of the projection, dodging among the rocks. Behind him, the two scalp hunters opened fire. Bullets hummed around Cole's ears. They whined off the rocks. Suddenly Cole's back and hips were drenched with water. One of the razor-sharp rock chips had shredded the water bag slung over his back. From below he heard a triumphal cry. The scalp hunters had seen.

Cole swore savagely. He was without water. He tried to go back and get Werdann's canteen.

Too late. Ballantine and Slocum had already reached Werdann's position. They fired at Cole and he was forced to retreat. He should have taken Werdann's canteen after he had killed him. That had been a stupid mistake — a white man's mistake — one that a real Apache would never have made, and Cole was afraid he was going to pay for it. You could never have too much water in this country.

He reached the base of the rock projection. A deep fissure in the granite led to the top. Cole slipped inside the fissure and began to climb. For the moment, he was hidden from the scalp hunters. The danger would come when he emerged on top. The water that dripped down his back cooled him in the heat. It was about the only use he would get from it.

He reached the top and climbed out, rolling as bullets spattered the rock around him. He took up a firing position. Ballantine and Slocum were in view below him, advancing. He fired at Ballantine. He heard an oath and saw the scalp hunter grab his ear. Then Ballantine and Slocum went to earth.

Cole shrugged off the punctured water skin and threw it away. The shirt that he had rolled around his waist was soaked. He took it off and began squeezing it into his mouth, sucking the water from the fabric, trying to get as much of the precious liquid into him before the shirt dried in the furnace-like heat. The water tasted salty from all the sweat that had soaked into the shirt. It was gritty with dirt.

There was a rifle shot. The bullet screamed off the face of the rock ledge. Cole heard distant footsteps, and looked out just in time to see Slocum running and diving for cover. It was too late to get a good shot at him, and Cole held his fire.

He continued sucking water from the shirt. He was going to be out here a long time, and this dirty water might mean the difference between life and death. He looked out. The scalp hunters were retreating back down the canyon, moving from cover to cover. Cole squeezed off a shot at Slocum. He missed, but the jowly scalp hunter dove awkwardly behind some rocks, and Cole heard a yelp.

"You hit?" Ballantine called.

"No, goddamn it," growled Slocum. "I landed in some cactus. One plant in this hell hole, and I got to fall on it."

Cole had gotten himself a commanding defensive position, but that was now irrelevant. The scalp hunters were doing the smart thing. They were doing what Cole would have done. They were moving to block Cole from the Tanks. There was no other water for a day's ride. Eventually Cole would have to go for water. He would have to go to the Tanks. He would have to go to Ballantine and Slocum.

"Hey, Cole!" It was Ballantine.

Cole didn't answer.

"Cole, it's awful hot out here, isn't it?"

Cole said nothing. Ballantine wanted him to reply. Shouting in this heat would make him thirstier.

Ballantine went on. "Cole, if you're thirsty, we've got enough water to go around. I'm having some right now, in fact. It sure is good." The scalp hunter's laughter rang off the canyon walls.

The sun beat down into the canyon with full force now. The rocks on which Cole lay were heating up. They wouldn't get hot enough to fry eggs — that was a myth — but they would get too hot for him to lie on.

He should find a patch of shade. He should hole up until dark, conserving himself, then make his move. That was what an Apache would do. Only an insane man — or a stupid one — would rush the scalp hunters in the daylight.

But Cole had only been adopted by the Apaches; he wasn't full-blooded. Those men out there had gotten his anger up. He wanted to kill them, and he didn't feel like waiting around all day to do it.

He put on the wet shirt. It would help to cool him for a bit. Then he picked up his rifle and went on the attack.

Chapter 27

The two scalp hunters had taken positions on either side of the canyon. Slocum was on the left, Ballantine on the right. The canyon slopes were a warren of boulders and crevices, providing good cover. Slocum was the weak link. Cole decided to work on him first.

Cole advanced from rock to rock, always making sure of his next move before he took it. He climbed the canyon wall, trying to get above Slocum. The two scalp hunters fired at him. Then they moved as well, back up the canyon, not wanting Cole to get behind them.

Cole went higher up the canyon wall. Slocum and Ballantine fired and moved back again. Despite all that he'd been through, Cole was in better shape than Slocum. He could move faster. He counted on these qualities to give him an advantage down the line.

Slowly, the fight moved back toward the Tanks. Cole advanced on Slocum. First Slocum fired at him, then Ballantine, while Slocum retreated to a better position. After a few minutes Cole moved again, with the same results. It was like an elegantly choreographed dance of death. The scalp hunters knew that Cole didn't have any water. Their strategy was to tire him out, to wear him down in the blistering heat.

It was a good strategy.

The water on Cole's shirt dried. His whole body dried. He sucked pebbles as he fought. Both scalp hunters had full canteens and they were retreating toward a source of water. Cole would have to kill them if he wanted to get a drink.

When Cole got a good shot at Slocum or Ballantine, he took it. He didn't take many, though. The Apaches had taught him to conserve ammunition. Both scalp hunters blazed away at Cole whenever he showed himself. Ballantine was the best shot, but he was farthest away. During one of Slocum's retreats, Cole wounded him, hitting him in the upper leg. The next time Cole saw the scalp hunter, he had tied his bandana around the wound.

Afternoon stillness descended on the canyon, the torpor disturbed only by an occasional flurry of gunshots that echoed off the rock walls. The three men drew nearer to the Tanks. The lure of the water was so great that Cole had to force himself to think what he was doing. He had to force himself not to go straight in and drink. In the heat, without a hat, with no water, he was beginning to suffer dizzy spells. He had to stop until the spells passed and he could go on once more.

When he had drawn nearly level with Slocum, he stopped running and began to crawl, wriggling unseen among the rocks and boulders. Slocum's last position had been on a rock overhang. Cole crawled past the overhang, inching along, then he worked his way down the canyon side. He hoped to take Slocum from the rear, to catch him looking the other way.

Crawling over the sharp, gravelly soil was agony on his injured chest, but he endured it. He moved slowly, watchfully, the hunting rifle cradled in the crook of his arms. The scalp hunters must be wondering where he had gone, what he was up to. Maybe they thought they'd hit him.

The rocks blocked almost all view as Cole neared the overhang. He licked his lips. His tongue was dry and raspy, like a cat's. He listened intently, heard nothing. He crawled closer. Slocum was still there; Cole smelled the man's rank odor.

Cole stood. With the Smith & Wesson leveled, he stepped around a rock and onto the overhang.

Slocum heard him and turned. Cole fired a fraction of a second before Slocum did. Slocum's bullet tore through Cole's shirt, grazing his ribs. Cole's bullet caught Slocum in the chest. "Ow!" said Slocum, doubling over. His rifle fell from his hands, off the overhang and down the steep slope to the canyon floor.

Slocum stumbled to his knees, holding his wound, trying to staunch the bleeding. There was blood on his bandaged leg, as well. He looked up at Cole and it was like they were comrades again. "Come on, Taggart. Give me a hand."

Slocum's eyes were pleading; Cole's eyes were cold. Cole placed a foot on Slocum's chest and pushed him off the overhang. The scalp hunter's screams rang through the canyon as he fell.

Slocum's canteen lay on the overhang. Cole picked it up. Fumbling with anticipation, he unscrewed the cap. Still holding his rifle, he raised the canteen to his lips.

There was a shot. The rifle was knocked from Cole's hand by the impact of the bullet, and the wooden canteen shattered. Cole ducked for cover. From the direction of the shot, he knew that Ballantine had crossed the canyon, then gotten above and behind him. He hadn't expected him to do that. Ballantine hadn't been wondering where Cole was; he'd had it figured out all along. He'd left Slocum out there as a decoy.

By a strange coincidence, Ballantine's bullet had hit the rifle and had been deflected into the canteen. The canteen had literally exploded from the bullet's impact. The rifle's receiver was smashed. Keeping the rifle in his hand had saved Cole's life. Otherwise, the bullet would have hit him.

Cole's hands and forearms dripped with water. He sucked them dry, getting what little of the precious moisture he could. From the rocks above, less than a hundred yards off, came Ballantine's boyish laughter. "Sorry about the water, Cole."

"Apologies noted," Cole cried back. He drew his pistol. He couldn't stay on the overhang. There was nowhere to maneuver. He'd be trapped, just as Slocum had been.

"It's just you and me now, Cole," Ballantine cried. "I don't want to shoot you."

Cole timed his move off the overhang. He dived behind a neighboring rock as Ballantine's bullet kicked up dirt just behind him.

"I thought we were friends," Ballantine went on.

"I thought so, too," Cole replied. "I reckon you were as close to a friend as I've ever had."

"Well, then, what's the matter? I saved your life twice, remember?"

"You also tried to kill me," Cole pointed out.

"You came here to kill me, too, remember that," said Ballantine. "So why don't we call it even and start over?"

"You killed Elena. That more than makes up for anything good you ever did."

"I didn't want to kill her."

"But you did. She trusted you, Ballantine. She didn't deserve to die like that."

"See it my way, will you? When we went back to the ant hills and you were gone, I knew right away she had set you loose. I knew she had fired those shots to make us think the Apaches were attacking. She admitted it, too, after we questioned her for a while. Hell, Cole, do you think I didn't know you and her were lovers? I know everything that goes on with my men. But I didn't care — don't you see? Because you were my *friend*."

Ballantine went on. "Elena had to die. I had no choice. Believe me, if there had been any other option, I would have taken it. But she had gone against the group. She had gone against *me*. If I hadn't killed her, no one would have listened to me anymore. But there is no more group, now. We can start over. You and me."

Cole had to keep going, he had to get some room to maneuver. He circled out from the rocks, moving uphill. Ballantine was moving, too. They saw each other. Ballantine fired his rifle at Cole. Cole wasted a pistol shot just to keep the scalp hunter's head down.

From out of sight, Ballantine said, "Come on, Cole. I've got a bag full of Apache scalps back there. You and I can split the money for them, fifty-fifty. We can take Slocum and Werdann in and collect the bounty on them, too. That's another thousand. Hell, we can say Werdann was me, if you want, and make it five thousand. That's a lot of money. What do you say?"

Cole kept circling up the hill. "No deal."

There was a brief pause, then Ballantine said, "I'm sorry to hear that, Cole, I really am. I'm going to hate killing you."

Cole's reply was a bullet that made Ballantine jump and move downhill, to new cover.

The two men stalked each other. Neither was sure where the other was. Cole had his pistol cocked and ready. He was at a disadvantage because Ballantine had the longer-range weapon. The sun beat down. The only sounds were Cole's hoarse breathing and the faint scraping of his moccasins against the gravel of the slope.

Cole could see the Tanks now, on their apron of worn rock. The sight of the Tanks heightened his thirst, but he couldn't go to the water without exposing himself and being shot. Neither could Ballantine, but Ballantine at least had some water left in his canteen.

Cole worked to his left and down, hoping to cut Ballantine off. But he didn't see him. He came back to the right, every sense alert, hand sweating on the pistol's wooden grip.

He heard a faint noise, below him and to the right.

He stopped. He didn't hear the noise again. There was no way of telling which way Ballantine was moving. For that reason, Cole couldn't circle the noise, the way an Apache would. He had to go straight toward it.

He inched along, hugging the hot face of a granite dome. He rounded a corner, pistol pointed. Ballantine rounded the dome at the same moment, not twenty yards off. Both men fired their weapons and ducked back behind cover. The gunshots and the whine of bullets off rock echoed through the canyon.

Cole studied the massive granite formation that separated him from Ballantine. He slipped his pistol into his belt and hoisted himself up the rock. He reached the top and squatted there, catching his breath and listening for Ballantine.

He heard nothing. He drew the pistol and moved across the

dome's uneven surface in a crouch. He moved silently, looking over the rock's top for Ballantine. He didn't see or hear him. Where was he?

Then he saw him, moving away from the dome, heading downhill toward the Tanks.

Cole started toward him, leveling his pistol. He must have made a noise, or else Ballantine had a sixth sense, because at that moment Ballantine looked up and saw him. Cole pointed the pistol and pulled the trigger.

Click. Misfire.

No time for another shot. Cole threw the pistol at Ballantine and leaped off the rock at him. The hurled pistol threw off Ballantine's reflex shot. Cole felt the rifle's hot blast on his cheek as he landed on the scalp hunter.

The two men rolled down the steep slope of the canyon, tearing clothes and skin, bouncing off sharp rocks. Cole landed about a quarter of the way from the bottom, near the Tanks. He shook his head, momentarily dazed. He tried to stand. Ballantine was a little above him. Ballantine got to his feet first. Ballantine's pistol had fallen from its holster in the roll down the hill. Ballantine picked up a rock and ran at Cole, swinging the rock at Cole's head.

Cole ducked, throwing himself at Ballantine's feet. Ballantine missed with the rock and went over Cole's back. Cole threw himself on the scalp hunter. They rolled the rest of the way down the hill. Ballantine got free. Cole got up and Ballantine put a shoulder into him, knocking him back down. Ballantine drew the knife from his belt. Cole's own knife was gone. Before Ballantine could set himself, Cole kicked the knife from his hand.

Instinctively, Ballantine looked to see where the weapon had gone. Cole charged him, catching him in the stomach, knocking him down. Ballantine used Cole's own momentum to throw Cole over onto his back.

Both men scrambled up. Ballantine hit Cole flush on the nose, breaking it. Cole felt blood run down his face. Ballantine swung at Cole again. This time Cole blocked the punch and followed with a right hand that rocked Ballantine.

Cole moved forward. Ballantine saw something, turned and ran for it. Cole saw it, too — sunlight glinting off metal. One of the pistols.

Cole ran after Ballantine. Just as Ballantine reached the pistol, Cole tackled him from behind. Both men went sliding forward in the dirt. Ballantine's outstretched hand reached for the pistol. Cole caught the hand. He knocked the pistol loose and flicked it out of the scalp hunter's reach. Ballantine rolled over and threw dirt at Cole's eyes. Cole ducked the dirt. He hit Ballantine in the face. He hit him again. Ballantine tried to fight back, but Cole overwhelmed him, with blow after blow after blow, until the scalp hunter was unconscious, blood covering his face.

Cole crawled off Ballantine, who moaned, stirring faintly. Cole was exhausted, dizzy, delirious from heat and thirst. He had to breathe through his mouth. Blood poured from his nose, but he was used to that. The nose had been busted so many times, it broke in a high wind anymore.

He looked around. The pistol had skidded onto the smooth rock at the edge of the Tanks. He crawled toward it. He picked up the pistol, cocking it, wanting to shoot Ballantine and get it over with. As he turned toward the scalp hunter, a pair of moccasined feet stepped in front of him.

Cole looked up. The feet belonged to an Apache Indian, and at first Cole thought that the Indian was part of his delirium. There was still a lot of black in the Indian's hair, though Cole knew that the man was at least seventy. The Indian's lined and wrinkled face looked down at Cole without pity. He wore a U.S. Army officer's jacket, unbuttoned, and a long breech clout. In one hand was a Winchester repeating rifle; at his waist was a Colt .45. He was accompanied by at least a dozen men, armed and painted for war.

Cole realized that the Indian was no dream, and he let out his breath. "Greetings, *Nantan*," he said. "Greetings, Chief."

Chapter 28

Nanay looked from Cole to Ballantine. The old chief was tall for an Indian, and frail looking now that Cole saw him up close. In the tribe he was called Broken Foot, because of a crippled ankle, but never to his face. Many said he was the greatest of all Apache war chiefs. He was responsible for far more white deaths than more celebrated leaders such as Cochise and Victorio.

The other Indians stood or squatted in the rocks, or in the cool shade of the ironwood tree. They were armed with rifles and pistols, and they looked ready, even eager, to use these weapons.

Cole didn't drop his pistol, nor did the Apaches tell him to. They didn't have to. They knew as well as he did that he had no chance to fight his way out of this. One shot was all he would get, if he was lucky, and then he would be dead.

Nanay turned his dark eyes back on Cole and nodded imperceptibly. "I did not expect to find the son of my old friend here." Apaches considered it rude to use personal names in addressing one another, except under certain unusual circumstances. Nanay had known Cole's adoptive father, Loco. The two men had been friends, but that friendship wouldn't keep Cole alive a second longer if Nanay decided that he should die.

Cole stood slowly. He had a hard time breathing because of his broken nose. He spit blood from his mouth; he wiped more blood on the back of his hand. He said, "How long were you watching, *Nantan?*"

"A long time," said the old man. "I like to watch the *nancin* fight among themselves."

The other Apaches laughed. *Nancin* was their warpath name for Americans or Mexicans.

Cole said "How did you get here?"

"We climbed the mountain. We followed your tracks." They must have left their horses on the other side of the mountain.

Cole looked at the unconscious Ballantine. "You know who that man is?"

"I know who he is. I know what he has done to my people. It is you that I wonder about. I wonder what the *yodascin* has become."

Cole knew that he was on trial, in a court every bit as powerful, and far more deadly, than any he might face in the white man's world. He said, "I was with those men, *Nantan*, it is true, but I was not one of them. I took no scalps. I pretended to be one of them in order to gain their confidence. It was I who warned your camp of the scalp hunters' attack. I came to this country to destroy their band. I came to avenge my father and the rest of my family who were killed by these men, as you will remember."

The old Apache took a turn around the rocks, limping with his arthritic stride. It must hurt him just to move, but he didn't show it. Cole couldn't imagine how he had scaled the mountain. Nanay was absolutely fearless. He knew that if Cole fought, he would be the first to die, yet he came back and stood inches from Cole. He said, "We followed two sets of tracks from the village of the Spanish priests. From the tracks, my people thought that the *nancin* were being followed by one of our own. I was not so sure. The moccasin prints were those of an Apache, but something in the stride reminded me of a white man. Now I see the *yodascin*, and I know why."

Cole said nothing.

Nanay went on, "The big yellow-hair at the Spanish village. You killed him?"

"Yes, *Nantan*."

"We found the remains of a woman, also. She was your woman?"

Cole hesitated. He might as well tell the truth. It would do no good to lie to a man like Nanay. But what was the truth?

"Yes, *Nantan*, she was mine. At least, she wanted to be mine, but I would not let her. She would have come with me if I had tried harder to make her. And because I did not try, she went back to this man" — he nodded toward Ballantine — "and he did . . . you saw what he did to her. Her fate was my responsibility."

"These men tortured you as well, did they not?" Nanay said.

"Yes, *Nantan*."

"Because of the woman?"

"Because they found out why I had come to them. It was the woman who saved me."

The old Indian looked closely at Cole, studying him. At last, he said, "All that you say may be true, my friend, or it may be that you were one of these people and had a falling out over the woman."

"That's right, Nanay," said a new voice. It was Ballantine, sitting up now. "It was all because of the girl. Taggart was one of us. He took as many scalps as any of us."

One of Ballantine's eyes was swollen shut. His face was bruised and puffy, and there was blood in his mouth. There was dried blood on his left shoulder, where his ear had bled after being grazed by Cole's bullet. He looked at Cole with a smug grin.

Nanay stared at Ballantine coldly, then turned away. The Apaches conferred among themselves. They seemed to be arguing, and Cole knew that boded ill for him. It would do him no good to beg for his life. It would even be counterproductive, for the Apaches would take it as a sign of guilt.

When the Indians had finished talking, Nanay turned back to Cole. Cole fingered the pistol in his sweaty hand. Nanay had such presence that Cole didn't think he would have the nerve to shoot him. Cole said, "What will you do with us, *Nantan?*"

Nanay nodded toward Ballantine. "*That* man we will take back to our camp. We will give him to our women. They may deal with him as they choose."

Cole's bowels went cold. Apache women were notoriously more ferocious than the men. The grin faded from Ballantine's face. He got to his feet. "No! No!" he begged. He looked to Cole for help.

Cole's words sounded as though they were coming from a great distance. "And me?"

Once more Nanay turned his wizened visage on Cole. The dark eyes looked into his. "These warriors say that you lie. They want you to suffer the same fate as the *nancin*. But I have always known my friend's son, the *yodascin*, to tell the truth. Whether they are correct or I, it is impossible to say. Therefore, we will let Ussen, Creator of Life, decide your fate."

He went on, "You shall be left here, without horse, or food, or weapons, or vessels to carry water. If you survive the desert, then *enjuh*, it is good. If not, you have lied to us."

Cole let out his breath. At least he had a chance. At least they weren't going to take him back to their camp. Better to die the torture of thirst on the *Jornada* than to die at the hands of the Apache women.

"Now, my friend, you must give me the pistol," Nanay ordered.

Panic stricken, Ballantine said, "Christ, Cole — don't let them do this to me. Shoot me. Kill me, please. Please God, Cole, I'm white, like you. Don't let them take me back to their women. You know what they'll do to me."

Cole didn't know, not for sure, but he could guess. It wouldn't be pretty, and it would take a long time. The ant hills would seem like a picnic in comparison.

Nanay seemed to read Cole's mind. Reluctantly, he said, "The *nancin* begs you to kill him. You know that, by our laws, you may claim that right. You were the victor in your fight with that man. It was a fair fight, and you have the right to dispose of him as you will. Either way, justice will be done."

Ballantine looked relieved. "Come on, Cole. Get it over with — before they change their minds."

Cole looked from Ballantine to Nanay, and back again.

"Hurry up, Cole," Ballantine said.

Cole let down the pistol's hammer.

Ballantine cried, "Cole!"

"Sorry," Cole said.

"Cole, think what they'll do to me."

"I am thinking. I'm thinking what you did to Elena, and to all those women and children back at the village, and to those Mexican sheepherders. And to my father and how many others?"

Ballantine moved forward, "Cole!"

With animal swiftness, the Apache warriors cut him off. They grabbed Ballantine's arms and dragged him away, to the draw where the horses waited. Ballantine struggled in the Indians' grasp. He looked back at Cole, and his once-boyish features were contorted with fear and rage. "I'll see you in hell, Taggart!" he cried.

"Like as not," Cole said. "But you'll get there first."

Cole faced Nanay and handed him the pistol.

The old Indian looked at Cole. For the first time, his dark eyes softened. "May we live long enough to meet each other again," he said.

Cole nodded in reply.

Nanay turned and left. In the background, Ballantine's terrified cries echoed above the Tanks.

The Apaches left the canyon with the blubbering Ballantine, taking the scalp hunters' horses with them, stopping to retrieve the white men's canteens and weapons.

Then they were gone and the sun beat down, and Cole was once again what he had always been, what he always would be — a Man Alone.

Cole drank from the Tanks and settled himself under the great ironwood tree. He would spend the night here. He would drink his fill and rest. Then, in the morning, he would begin his long walk back to civilization.

Ignacio Cruz would be surprised to see him.

ABOUT THE AUTHOR

Robert Broomall is the author of eighteen published novels. Besides writing, his chief interests are travel and history, especially military history, the Old West, and the Middle Ages.

Amazon author page:
https://www.amazon.com/author/robertbroomall

Amazon Kindle page:
http://www.amazon.com/s/ref=nb_sb_noss_1?url=search-alias%3Ddigital-text&field-keywords=Robert+Broomall

Blog: http://www.rwbroomall.com

Made in the USA
Monee, IL
17 July 2022